Life of Sin

Lock Down Publications and Ca$h
Presents
Life of Sin
A Novel by *T.J. & Jelissa*

Life of Sin

Lock Down Publications

P.O. Box 870494
Mesquite, Tx 75187

Visit our website @
www.lockdownpublications.com

Copyright 2019 Life of Sin

Lock Down Publications
Like our page on Facebook: Lock Down Publications @
www.facebook.com/lockdownpublications.ldp
Cover design and layout by: **Dynasty Cover Me**
Book interior design by: **Shawn Walker**
Edited by: **Kierra Northington**

Stay Connected with Us!

Text **LOCKDOWN** to 22828 to stay up-to-date with new releases, sneak peaks, contests and more…

Thank you.

Submission Guideline.

Submit the first three chapters of your completed manuscript to ldpsubmissions@gmail.com, subject line: Your book's title. The manuscript must be in a .doc file and sent as an attachment. Document should be in Times New Roman, double spaced and in size 12 font. Also, provide your synopsis and full contact information. If sending multiple submissions, they must each be in a separate email.

Have a story but no way to send it electronically? You can still submit to LDP/Ca$h Presents. Send in the first three chapters, written or typed, of your completed manuscript to:

LDP: Submissions Dept
Po Box 870494
Mesquite, Tx 75187

DO NOT send original manuscript. Must be a duplicate.

Provide your synopsis and a cover letter containing your full contact information.

Thanks for considering LDP and Ca$h Presents.

T.J. & Jelissa

Note to Readers:

We sincerely thank you all for rocking with us. Thank you for your continued support. Thank you for downloading, purchasing, reviewing and/or sharing our books. Most importantly, we want thank God for his covering and blessings he's rained down upon our family. It is because of Him, that we are able to do what we do.

Please stay connected with us on Facebook: https://www.facebook.com/MrsTJEdwards or join our reading group: https://www.facebook.com/groups/Feenin4Fiction/ to stay up to date on our latest releases, giveaways and more.

Love Always,
T.J. and Jelissa

"...please, just trust me."

T.J. & Jelissa

Life of Sin

Chapter 1

Jade

Crash!

Dishes shattered, spewing glass across the hardwood floor. I opened my bedroom door and peeked down the narrow hallway, into the living room, terrified to step out the confines of my safety and into the warzone my father created.

My knees shook, almost too weak to hold me up. Sweat slid down the side of my face. A lone tear dripped southward, traveled until it fell off my chin and on to the carpet. The lump in my throat that felt like the size of a golf ball, made it difficult to swallow. I dared to stick my head further out of the room.

In the back of my mind, I knew that my decision to make my presence known could cause me to wind up on the receiving end of my father's drunken wrath as it had so many times before. From my vantage point, I could see my beautiful mother run across the living room before my father, Leon, grabbed her by her short afro and pulled her back to him. Even from the distance I stood, I could hear his words clearly.

"Bitch, I'm tired of yo shit, and I'm tired of providing for these punk-ass kids. I want you to pack only the stuff you brought, and get the hell out of my house before I kill you. I swear to God, I ain't gon tell you again," he promised, tightening his grip in her hair.

My mother tilted her head backward. Tears fell from her small, beautiful face. Her lips were already split from his assaults. She swallowed and dared to plead her case. "Leon, where I'm gon go? Huh? I ain't got no money. And you made me leave all of my family back in New York. Everything I have, and everything me and these kids depend on, comes through you."

He tightened his grip and yanked her head back to him. "Bitch, I ain't ask you all of that. Now, get them kids and get out of my house." He threw her to the floor and kicked her right in her backside. "Go wake them kids up and get 'em out of my house. I can't take this shit no more!" He picked up the glass table in the middle of the living room, brought it just above his forehead, and slammed it down as hard as he could, breaking it into a hundred pieces. "Now, Macy! Get out!"

My mother yelped and scooted backwards on her backside. "It's below zero outside. I ain't had the money to buy the kids no coats suitable for the winter. I beg of you, please don't do this. Don't do this to us. You're all we have." She slowly came to her feet, her arms outstretched, walking toward him. "Leon, how can I make you feel better? What can I do for you?" she asked in a calm, yet shaky voice. "Please, baby, I'll do anything."

I shook my head as I ventured further into the hallway, searching for the courage to rescue my mother, to walk into the living room and convince her to leave this man's house. The courage to get her to see that my father, Leon, caused us more harm than good, with his abusive behaviors. I wished I had the courage to stand up to him. To tell him he was a horrible man, and that no man should have done to their family all he had. I wished I had the courage to fight beside my mother in the times when he got physically abusive. But, I was afraid, and only a young woman of eighteen. Weighed a hundred and twenty-five pounds, and had never had a fight in by entire life. There was no way I could stand up to a man of six feet four inches, weighing two hundred and sixty pounds. I'd been on the ass end of his blows before and found myself waking up after a short slumber. No, my father had killed my courage a long time ago. My courage, my self-esteem, my self-worth, my faith in God, and my faith in the fact that one day, things would get better. I was broken and had been since the age of fourteen, when he'd hurt me worse than I could have ever imagined.

His hand rose in the air and backhanded my mother so fast and so hard, she flew against the wall. Before she could slide down to the floor, he yanked her back up and slapped her again.

WHAP!

Then, he threw her to the floor, kicking her in the side. "Go wake them fucking kids up and get out of my house! If you don't, I'ma kill you and them. Now, try me, Macy! I swear to God, I ain't playing wit you." He pulled a long knife from his inside coat pocket, and held it at his side. From where I stood, I could see the light gleam off the blade.

I took off running down the hallway, and fell beside my mother, no longer caring what he would do to me for assisting her. I had to get her out of there and to safety. I knew he had it inside him to really kill her, and I couldn't allow that to happen. In my heart, my mother was all I had. The only person in the world I felt really cared about me, and my twin sisters, Ashley and Ashland. When I knelt beside her, she appeared dazed and out of her mind. I grabbed her shoulders. "Mama, come on, let's just get out of his house. Please, let's just go before somebody gets hurt." I looked over my shoulder at my father, as a bottle of Jack Daniels appeared in his hands. He twisted the cap off, threw it to the floor and turned the bottle up, guzzling like a true alcoholic. I shook my mother's shoulders. "Mama, please get up."

She pushed my hands away and staggered to her feet as blood fell from her nose. She touched it with the tip of her index finger, looked down at it and her eyes bucked, then lowered into slits. "I'm tired of you putting your hands on me, Leon. Every day, you gotta find a reason to put your no-good, filthy hands on me, and I'm sick of it!" she hollered, balling her fists. Tears ran down her cheeks in rivulets.

My father snickered, then drained the rest of the liquor from the bottle. Twirled his tongue around the opening of it, and threw it to the floor. The bottle bounced up and wound up rolling against the wall. He burped as loud as he could, and laughed. "Bitch, you don't think fat meat greasy, do you?" He pulled his shirt over his head and tossed it to the floor. "Jade, get yo ass back in that room, because I'm about to kick the dog shit out of yo mama. I'm tired of this bitch playing wit me." He mugged her, then looked down to me. "Gone, get now, lil girl!"

"Mama, please come with me. I am begging you. Nobody needs to be hurt. He's drunk. He doesn't know what he's doing right now. Let's just go," I pleaded.

My mother wiped the blood from her mouth and nose. She took a deep breath and swallowed. "Nall, baby. I'm tired of bowing down to a man that don't give two fucks about me, or the children I nourished inside of my body for him. The buck stops here. We ain't going nowhere. If anybody is leaving tonight, it's him. This is my house. I ain't going on into that cold. Not tonight, not tomorrow, not ever!" she screamed at him.

My knees were shaking so bad, I feared I was seconds away from falling on my face. I was terrified for my mother, myself and my sisters. I knew my father's temper was lethal. He was impulsive. Had a habit of reacting and causing as much bodily harm as possible, before he calmed down and recognized what he'd done. As crazy as it sounds, I felt my mother was provoking the crazy out of him, in a way. Antagonizing him and luring the psycho out of him. I just wanted for us to leave the small project apartment in the Red Hook Houses. I was tired of Brooklyn anyway. Tired of the same old, same old. The dope addicts, the prostitutes, the robbers, the swindlers, the gang bangers, and the shootings. It was more dangerous trying to walk the halls of our projects, than it was actually being outside in the streets of East New York. Leaving my father would be more of a benefit, than a downfall.

"Mama, please just come on, let's just—" Before I could finish my next sentence, my father grabbed me by my locks, and yanked my head back so far, I heard a snapping sound. He threw me to the floor and kicked me so hard in the stomach that he knocked the wind out of me. I let out a gust of air, and regurgitated portions of my lunch all over the floor. The kick hurt so bad I was seeing stars. I lay on my side is agony.

"I know you love these kids. You wanna play these games wit me, I'll make them pay for your sins." He cocked his right foot back and brought it forward, right into my back. "Get out my house."

His kick flipped me onto my chest. I was crying and struggling to breathe, trying my all to come to a push-up position, so I could crawl out the living room. My head was spinning. My heart beat rapidly in my chest. I hated life for allowing this to happen to me. *What girl deserved this punishment? Why had I been born?* I found myself often questioning the heavens above.

My father went to kick me again, but my mother jumped onto his back, and bit him on the side of the face as hard as she could. She wrapped her arms around his neck. Her bare feet interlocked under his chest.

"Arrgh! Arrgh! Get this bitch off of me before I kill her! Arrgh!" He ran backwards into a wall, crashing her into it. Her mouth pried loose from his cheek for a split second, and then she bit into him again. This sent my father running into the kitchen. He crashed into the refrigerator, hollering. Blood dripped from where my mother's teeth were deep inside his jaw.

I used the wall to help myself come to a standstill. My ribs felt like they were bruised, and maybe even broken. My breathing ragged, labored. The room seemed to be spinning like a tornado. I saw one of my dreadlocks on the floor, the mini seashell still attached to it. Looking into the kitchen, my father reached behind himself, and grabbed ahold of my mother's nightgown, tearing the cheap material, exposing her nakedness underneath. He'd stormed into the house just before she'd been able to take her nightly bath.

"Leave, Leon. Leave me and these kids alone. Just go, since you don't want to be a husband and father no more. I'll figure it out on my own. Please," she cried. My mother was usually a quiet and reserved woman. She stood at five feet three inches tall, a hundred and thirty pounds, with light caramel skin, and freckles strategically placed by God all over her face. Freckles she'd passed down to me and my twin sisters. For as long as I had been alive, I had never witnessed her fighting my father back. I felt she'd had enough. That she'd reached her wit's end of things.

Somehow, someway, my father flipped her off his back and slammed her on top of the stove. She hollered out in pain as soon as her back landed on one of the cooking guards covering one of the four eyes. Her face contorted into one of intense pain. This left her vulnerable. My father grabbed her by the throat and began to squeeze. A thick vein appeared in the middle of his forehead. He added a second hand, choking her. "Die, bitch, I told you. Die." His hands seemed to vibrate as he choked my mother before me, squeezing tighter and tighter and tighter. Slob dripped from the corner of his mouth.

I fought through the pain and rushed over to him as fast as I could. "Daddy. Daddy. Please stop. You're killing my mama. You're killing her. Stop." I tried to pry his huge hands from her throat, but doing so only seemed to fuel his rage. Her gagging intensified. Her arms went limp at her sides. This terrified me.

"Yeah, bitch, I told you. I told you I was gon kill that ass. Now die. Die now!" He started to break into a maniacal laughter. His mouth was wide open, a sinister look spread across his face. He appeared to be taking delight in his demonic handy work. What kind of man looked to beat down and murder the mother of his children, the wife God had provided him? Life had a way of showing me it was more dark than light. More hate than love.

I looked around in search for a weapon. Anything that would help me to assist my mother out of the sticky situation she was in. In my opinion, my father looked to kill her. He looked to end her life, and I could only imagine either myself, or my sisters were next. The thought of it terrified my soul, but I couldn't allow the fear to freeze me. I had to help my mother. Had to free her from his murderous grip, and get her, myself and my siblings to safety. So I searched and scanned the house until my eyes fell upon the lamp sitting on top of the living room table. It was my only hope. One glance inside the kitchen told me my mother was barely hanging on for dear life. Her eyes rolled into the back of her head. Her face was a bluish-brown hue. It was now or never.

I grabbed the lamp from the table, unplugged it, and ripped the shade from it. Wrapped the cord around the body, and ran as fast as my injured ribs would allow me, back into the kitchen and raised it over my head with tears running down my face. "Daddy, please let my mother go. You're killing her. You're killing her," I cried, trying to muster the moxie to do what was needed next.

"This bitch is dead. She's dead. I told her to stop playing wit me!" he snapped, choking my precious mother with as much strength as he could. Her body appeared limp as her knuckles rested on the floor with her mouth agape. The fight within her had died. She'd had all she could take.

I raised the lamp as high as I could, and brought it down on the back of his head.

Bam!

It shattered in my hands, the glass cutting into my fingers and my palms. I was left holding a silver-like pole from inside the lamp.

He dropped her and fell to his knees. His face landed between his legs. He groaned in pain. "Aw, bitch. What did you do? Oh, my God, what did you do?" Blood oozed out of the wound and poured down his neck like Louisiana hot sauce. He grabbed the top of the stove and forced himself upward.

I backed up with my hands held at shoulder length. "Daddy, I'm sorry. I'm sorry, but you were killing my mother. I couldn't let you kill her." I continued to walk backward, scared for my life. I knew I was in for a hell of a beating, at the very least.

He winced and turned to me. "You lil bitch. You just like yo mama. Well, to the grave with you too then." He stood straight up and rushed me. Grabbed ahold of my neck, and picked me up in the air. Slammed my back against the wall, and placed his forehead against mine. "I wanted you to stay wit me, baby. All you had to do was mind your bidness, and Daddy would have done you right." He rested his lips against mine and began to choke the life out of my body.

Instead of fighting him, I close my eyes and welcomed death. What could life possibly have in store for me? Ever since I'd been five years old my father had been beating me, and verbally assaulting me. Since the age of thirteen, he'd been forcing himself upon me whenever he felt like it. Beating my mother down in front of me and my sisters, and whenever he got tired of beating her, he took his anger and violence out on his children. So, what did life have to possibly grant me, other than more forms of pain? I squeezed my eyes tighter and begged for Jehovah to take me away and allow me and my mother to meet back up in heaven. Begged him to keep my sisters safe and sound and if he couldn't, to bring them along with us in the most pain-free way as possible. I felt the life leaving my body. Felt myself getting numb, when my father hollered out and dropped me to the floor, just as two big rats ran from under the stove and towards the back of the house.

I opened my eyes and looked up in time to see my mother with a bloody knife in her hand. She took it and slammed it into his back again, then pulled it out and held it, looking down at him. He fell to his face shaking on the floor. His eyes bugged out of his head. My mother dropped to her knees. "What have I done? Oh my God, what have I done?" she cried, falling beside him, rolling his body over and hugging him, while his blood saturated her torn nightgown.

Chapter 2

Bentley

"Ssh, be quiet, and come on while your daddy still sleeping," Asia advised, pulling me by the wrist and leading me toward the back door to our apartment. Asia was my father's second wife, and the mother-to-be of his kid. She was two months pregnant, and her hormones were already raging. My pops was forty-one and Asia was thirty-four, high yellow with green eyes, about five feet six inches tall, and every bit of a hundred and forty pounds. Around the Red Hook Housing Projects, she was known back in the day for being a straight-up gold digger, and a bit of a ho. How my old man had managed to turn her into a housewife, and put a baby in her tummy was beyond me. I didn't ask questions, the only thing I was concerned about was that gap between her legs.

We crept down the back stairwell until we got to the ninth floor. Once there, we took the hallway and wound up at her front door she'd left slightly ajar. She kept ahold of my wrist and pulled me inside. Before the door was even closed she grabbed me to her, kissing then sucking all over my lips loudly. The scent of her perfume drifted up my nose. She smelled sweet and forbidden. Hugged me close, breathing heavy. "Damn, Bentley, I been thinking about giving you some of this pussy all day long. It took forever for your daddy to fall asleep." She sucked on my neck and moaned deep within her throat.

My hands slid around and cuffed her big ass. She had to be every bit of forty inches back there. She was what we referred to in Brooklyn as "Project Strapped." That ass was fatter than Santa Claus's belly, and my hands were all over it. She had on this short skirt that clung to her curves. Every time I released her booty, it sprung back into place after jiggling for a split second. Asia was bad, and even though I often felt bad about smashing my Pops' wife, the sight and feel of her body always pushed me over the hump. I was so hard my piece was sticking above my waistband, with the head throbbing, ready to feel her forbidden heat. My hand slid under the hem, connecting with hot skin. "Yo, you got what I need to get right, though?" I slid all the way under her ass cheeks, until I was playing around in her crease. She was without panties. Her lips were puffy and saturated with her dew. The feel of her sap got me excited. I dared to slide a finger into her hole, her lips wrapped around it right away.

"Unn. Yeah, lil daddy. You know I got you. When have I ever let you down?" she asked, backing into my finger, swallowing it. Her teeth scraped my neck, then she was sucking on it again.

I backed her into the wall face-first, knelt down and pulled her skirt above her waist, exposing her golden colored ass cheeks, with slight stretch marks along them that I could only see when I as close to her as I was. For me, it made her that much more sexy. I had a thing for older women, and it was all because of her. "Spread them mafucking legs, ma, you know what time it is." I slid my hand up the inside of her thighs, all the way up to her dripping box. The closer I got to her goody box, the hotter the region became.

She spread her legs, and tried to look down at me. "Damn, Bentley, what you about to do to me now?" She placed her hands on the wall, and bit into her bottom lip. Her green eyes peered into mine.

I stuffed my face into the apex of her thighs. Sniffed hard, took my tongue and licked up and down her sex lips, sucked them into my mouth, popped them out, and spread them wide, attacking her vagina's nipple with my tongue, while my eyebrows rested on her ass's soft ample ass cheeks. "Damn. Damn. There you go. There you go. You always doing this shit to me. Yes, aw fuck yes, lil daddy." She reached under herself and spread her pussy lips for me, her clit popped out like the tip of a pinky finger.

I trapped it with my lips, sucked hard, just like she'd taught me, then twirled my tongue around it repeatedly. My hands ran up and down her thick thighs, squeezing them. I was obsessed with feeling all over her. I could taste her essence in the back of my throat and on my tongue. It added fuel to my already raging inferno. I slid my tongue in and out of her at full speed, praying for her to cum on it.

"Bentley, smack my ass like you always do. Smack it and keep on eating me please. Fuck. Please, lil daddy." Now, her fingers were playing in her lap crazily. They were moving so fast, they became a blur. Her essence dropped from them and onto the stained carpet. "Uh!"

I smacked that ass hard. Watched it jiggle, then smacked it again, before trapping her pearl with my lips. Once there, my tongue flicked back and forth across it, over and over. Her thighs began to shake. She bucked, and humped back into my face. I got to vacuuming her lips, sucking them in and popping them out, sliding my tongue in between them again, assaulting her clitoris.

"Uh, fuck you, Bentley. Uh, you always doing somethin'." She screamed and sank to the ground, shaking with her eyes closed tight.

I got down and kissed all over her ass, playing with her pearl, while I stroked my shaft up and down and grabbed her by the hair. "Bitch, raise that thigh so I can get in this pussy." I smacked her on that ripe ass.

She yelped. "Uh! Yes, lil daddy." She raised her thigh to her rib cage, and held her pussy lips open for me. "Come on, baby."

I held my pipe in my right hand, and guided him slowly into her box. Her juices were oozing out of her. Her heat seared me inch by inch, until I filled her with all of me. Then, I was stroking fast and deep, while her calf rested in the crook of my arm. That juicy booty shook every time I slammed forward. I sucked on her neck. "Tell me you love this shit. Tell me you love your husband's son fucking you." I scooted closer and got to really hitting her goodies.

Clap. Clap. Clap. Clap.

"Un. Un. Un. Un. Uh. Yes. Oooo. Yes. I love my hubby. Uh. I love my hubby, son. Uh-shit. Fucking me like this! Uh, I'm finna cum already. Damn, that dick got me!" She arched her back and let out a piercing scream. Scratched at the carpet, and bounced back into me over and over again. That was one of the things I loved about Asia, she was a screamer. It made me feel like a straight don, to have a grown-ass woman getting impaled on my dick and hollering at the top of her lungs like I was killing her. On top of that, her pussy was so wet. I was slipping in and out of it with no effort. Her grip was right though. Tugging on me like a closed fist. My pops' wife had some bomb-ass pussy and I was trying to go as deep into it as I could. She reached behind her and held my waist, so she could feel me crashing into her sweet spot.

I bit into the back of her neck, growling, popping my hips forward, thrusting faster and faster. My breathing intensified. Every time her skin slapped into mine, it sent chills through me, brought me closer and closer to the brink of my climax. "Asia. Asia. Damn, ma, I'm bout to cum. I'm 'bout to cum in this pregnant ass pussy. Shit." I raised her thigh into the air, crashing into her body with no remorse.

She dug her nails into the side of my backside, and scratched me. "Cum in me, Bentley. Cum in me. I swear, I swear, it's good! Uh, shit, young-ass nigga. Cum in me now!" She pushed back into my lap as hard as she could, her sandy brown hair falling into and covering her face. It had grown more than four inches since she'd been pregnant. She made a habit of bragging about it ever chance she got.

I slid my hand under her shirt, and squeezed her right breast. The nipple poked into the palm of my hand. The feel of it and her bouncing back into my lap, became too much. I sucked her neck, and came deep within her channel. Jerking, and ramming her womb, digging as deep as I could, loving the way her walls closed in on me. "Huh. Huh. Huh. Mmm-shit." I fell against her back, still eight and a half inches deep.

Her face remained in the carpet. Her eyes were closed tight. Her tongue traced over her luscious lips. "Get off of me, Bentley. Let me taste us. You know I love how we taste."

I pulled out, my piece glossy with her juices and laid on my back, still breathing hard. She climbed onto her knees and kissed all over my exposed abs, after lifting my white beater up to my chest. "I'ma get you right, lil daddy. I was able to catch my brother slipping. I hit his stash and what I got, you should be able to make at least three gees. Just hit the light bill for me, and spend tomorrow night with me and we good. Rent ain't due for another four weeks, so..." She took my dick in her fist, and licked her lips, pumped him up and down, then took her tongue from the bottom of him, and licked all the way to the top. "Mmm." Closed her eyes, and sucked me into her mouth. Swallowed me all the way to my sack, then pulled her lips back. "That sound like a plan, lil daddy?"

T.J. & Jelissa

My toes curled inside my AirMax. Eyes rolled into the back of my head. Asia's head was always the best for me. Not that I had too many females to compare it to, but the ones I did, she was crushing them by a long shot. Her head is what kept my lil young ass hooked. Every time she licked her lips around me, I found myself trying to find a duck-off spot so I could watch her handle her bidness in all her splendor.

"Yeah, shorty. That shit sound one hunnit. Make me cum again. I wanna see you swallow me.'"

She moaned around my piece, and really got to doing her thing, slurping all loud and shit. She had my piece so wet, her slit oozed down my shaft and settled around my sack. I gave her ass an A-plus, and came down her throat, humping up from the floor. She tightened her fist, and stroked me up and down, then rubbed it all over her face, before sitting on her haunches. Her tongue circled her lips. "Dang, yo lil ass got me whipped. Get up, so I can show you what's good." She stood up, and reached for me.

I grabbed her hand, then came to my feet, stretching my hands over my head. My piece stood straight up, glistening with her spit all over it. "Yo, I need to jump in this shower real quick. Then I gotta go and buss a move wit Santana. Kid, on one and I'm tryna be on one with him." I said this, stepping past her and into the bathroom. One thing I didn't like about Asia was that she wanted to hug up wit me every time I after I hit that pussy. I wasn't wit all that lovey-dovey shit. Once I came, I liked to be on my way. I had that money on my mind like crazy. But, I also didn't like roaming around smelling like sex either, so I had my mind dead set on getting as fresh as I could before I hit up the slums. I could have gone back to me and my old man's place, but I was feeling guilty after fucking his wife, so I decided to shower down at her crib, then hit the bricks. I had a quota of bringing in no less than a $1,000 a day and being that it was already twelve in the afternoon, I felt like I was behind.

Asia waited until I turned the dials on the shower, before she came from behind me, and hugged me from the back. "But, bayy-bee, I thought you was gon lay up and chill wit me for a minute? You know how I get and shit after you gimme that magic stick. Damn, why you acting all brand new?" She squeezed me, and tried to turn me around to face her.

I kept on adjusting the water temperature until I got it right. Then, I dropped the remainder of my clothes, and stepped into the water. The flow cascaded onto my chest, popping all over the place. "Shorty, I ain't ducking wit you. If you wanna hug up wit a nigga, go holler at my pops. You his bitch, not mine. I gave you all you getting for the day. Leave that work on top of my pants out there, so I can snatch it up before I bounce. Straight up." I closed the curtain, and stuck my head all the way under the current. Closed my eyes, and allowed the shower to take me to a serene place.

"I swear to God, Bentley, you be tryna treat me like one of them bum-ass bitches out here in Brooklyn. On everything, I ain't gon keep geeing for that oil, boy. That's my word." She said this and stomped out of the bathroom. I could hear her talking to herself the entire time I was getting clean, but when I came out of the bathroom, she had the three thousand dollars' worth of work sitting on top of my pants, just as I'd directed her.

***

Fifteen minutes later, I got dressed and threw on my AirMax, just as my father, wearing his mechanic's uniform, opened the door to her apartment and let himself in. My father stood at five feet eleven inches tall, was dark skinned, and weighed at least a hundred and eighty pounds. He was built solid, and had a low cut, with graying waves on top of his head. When he saw I was there, he frowned, then looked over my shoulder toward the back of the small apartment. "Where is Asia? She in the back room?" He stepped all the way inside, and closed the door behind him. He had his uniform unzipped halfway down, so his gut could hang out. His Timbs were stained with motor oil.

I nodded, avoiding eye contact with him. "Yeah, she back there. I think she might be on her way to sleep. I know she been complaining about having a major migraine all day," I lied. I said it loud enough for her to corroborate the story. I didn't know what else to possibly say to him, because I knew I was in the wrong. There was no reason I should have been screwing his pregnant wife, but there I was, less than a half-hour earlier, digging all in her guts. "Yo, I'm about to head out. I should be back at like ten or so. I'ma stroll through and check on my mother too. You want me to tell her anything?" I knew that was a dumb question. My father and my mother had separated on the worst possible terms. She'd caught him in the bed twice with Asia, found out that he'd been cheating on her for over two years, and the stress of it all drove my mother unto a destructive path of crack cocaine. I'd watched her in the span of six months go from one of the most beautiful women I'd ever laid eyes on, to a woman of barely ninety pounds, sunken and lost. Every time I saw my mother these days, it was a task not to break down in front of her. A major part of me blamed my father for her downward spiral, and I guess it was one of the reasons I'd been fucking Asia every chance I got. And, it had been since the day my father walked out on my mother.

He ran his hands over his waves. Shook his head. "Son, I ain't got nothing to say to that woman. Our lines have been drawn in the sand. We know where we stand, and that's just that. Besides, I don't know the woman she's become. I really don't." He scratched his scalp and looked at his nails, before popping the dandruff out of them. "Son, what were you doing here?"

I shrugged my shoulders. "Chilling. Santana was supposed to be here already. This where I told him to meet me at, because I know you don't like him meeting me at our crib, ever since y'all got into that fight over his mother. But, he ain't got here yet, so I'm just cooling." I stepped past him. Why?"

He looked me over from the corner of his eye, then shook his head. "No reason, just asking, that's all. Anyway, bring a pizza home tonight and leave me a few slices. Don't have that lil thirsty nigga all in my crib either."

I could've argued the fact that I paid half of all the bills, but I decided against it. I could still feel his bitch's scratch marks all over my back, so I decided to let him have this one. I nodded, and stepped out of the door and into the hallway with a slight grin on my face. It was time to get money. I pulled out my iPhone X and called up my mans, Santana, ready to hit the block up. Kept the phone glued to my ear, opened the door to the stairwell and dropped the phone. "What the fuck?"

T.J. & Jelissa

Chapter 3

Jade

I never knew my mother was so heavy. I had one arm draped around her neck, and trying to hold her up. She was hysterical after the reality of what she'd done to my father finally came and hit her. She ran around the apartment screaming, "Oh my God, what have I done? What have I done? I just killed the love of my life. What have I done?" She screamed it so loud, I was sure some of the neighbors had heard her. It took nearly five minutes for me to calm her down. Even then, she kept repeating what she'd done over and over again, freaking me out.

We slumped to the floor in the hallway together, hugged up, fearing the worst. "Mama, we gotta get out of here. We gotta get out of here or they're going to throw both of us in jail," I cried, imagining being separated from my mother. I couldn't believe my little sisters had managed to sleep through all the commotion. But, when my mother got to running around the house like a chicken with its head cut off, they finally woke up and started to cry, and call my mother's name. "We gotta get out of here, Mama. Please listen to me." I waved my little sisters over. They were both peeking out of their bedroom door. I could see the fear written all over their faces.

My mother was covered in blood and now, so was I. "I can't believe I did what I did to him. I'm so stupid. I'm so stupid. He was all we had!" She jumped up, ran into the kitchen, and lay on the floor on top of him, crying and hugging his body. "I'm so sorry, baby. Please don't die. Please, come back to me. I'ma go and get you some help." She jumped up and looked as if she was possessed. Her eyes were bucked. Sweat and blood was all over her face. Her short afro was curled up and matted on one side. Her gown was barely hanging on, because it had been ripped so badly, and what was left of the material was caked in blood. She looked like she'd stepped right out of a horror movie. "Gotta go get my baby some help." She ran to the door and twisted the knob, pulled it back, and the chain snapped loudly. "Open up, you son of a bitch. Open up right now. Please."

I slowly walked up to her, and placed my hands on her shoulders. This made her jump and snap her head back to me. "Mama, calm down, you're scaring the twins. Please, let's get you in some clothes. Then, we're going to get the hell out of here. You, me and the twins."

"No!" she screamed, turning around and pushing me as hard as she could. I flew backward and tripped over my own feet. I fell hard, the back of my head ricocheting off the hard floor. "You selfish bitch. I gotta go get some help for my man! Get out of my way, all of this is your fault!" She ran back into the kitchen and picked up the knife, then walked toward me with it at her side. "You made me do this, Jade. You did. He would have never been beating my ass if you had given him everything he wanted. You could have kept us happy. Now, my baby is gone. Bitch, I'ma kill you!" She rushed at me with the knife, hollering like a maniac.

"Holy shit!" I hopped up and almost broke my neck, trying to get out of that living room and down the hallway to safety. Ashley had just started to come down the hall, calling for our mother. I grabbed her, picked her up and carried her into the bedroom, before slamming the door in my mother's face.

She beat on the door for two minutes straight. "Open this door, Jade. Open this door. All of this is your fault. You did this! You did this!" After more beating, she snapped and started to stab the door over and over. "I hate you! I hate you, Jade! I know what y'all was doing behind my back. This is your fault! It's your fucking fault. I'll never forgive you for this!" She jiggled the door handle, then sank to the floor. I could hear her sobbing loudly.

Ashley ran to me and hugged my waist. "What's the matter with our mother, Jade? Why is she trying to kill us?" she cried, holding me tight.

Ashland looked on from a short distance with her eyes wide. Out of the twins, she was the quiet, more introverted one. Tears fell down her cheeks. She reached out to me, and I pulled her close to my body. "I'm scared, Jade. I'm scared."

I knelt down so I could hug both of them at one time. "It's okay, we're going to be okay. Mama is just dealing with something right now. She'll be good in a second."

"Fuck, I gotta get my husband some help!" The door rattled, and then I could hear her heavy footsteps rushing down the hallway. "I'm going to go get some help, Leon! Don't worry, baby! I gotchu!" There was a loud clanking sound. "Ahh, open the door, fucking chain!"

I wiped my tears away and continued to hold my sisters. "Look, I want you girls to stay in this room and do not open this door for nobody, do you understand me?" I looked from one five-year-old twin, to the next. They were spitting images of myself.

"I'm scared, Jade. Where are you finna go?" Ashley whimpered, holding onto me tighter.

"I'll be back, just do what I say. Don't open this door for nobody. I mean that."

"Not even Mama?" Ashland asked, just to be sure.

"Not even Mama." I kissed both of them on their cheek, and slowly unlocked the door by using of the knob. Pulled it open, then peeked down the narrow hallway. Two mice ran in my direction, and before they could get close to me, they took a detour and ran into my parents' room screeching loudly. My mother had just opened the front door with the knife in her hand. Her entire gown had fallen around her ankles. She opened the door and ran out. I took off in pursuit of her. "Mama! No!" I started to imagine her being in prison for the rest of her life and it freaked me out. I couldn't let that happen. I had to find a way to get her back on track, so we could get the hell out of Brooklyn. Since my birth, the city had been nothing but one of pain and torture for me, and my family as a whole. I felt that if we could get out of the city, we could start over somewhere new, and without the demonic leadership of my father. The comments my mother had made about some of the things he'd forced me to take part in had hit me hard, but this moment wasn't the time for me to dwell on it. I had to save her, had to get to her before somebody else did. She was out of her mind. Deranged and mentally in shock by what had taken place with my father.

When I got into the hallway, she was just rushing into the stairwell door, talking to herself. Her naked body was on full display for all the world to see, along with the injuries that my father had caused her by his beating. "Mama!" I ran after her, my bare feet slapping the concrete in the hallway as I sprinted as fast as I could. I got to the door and pushed it open, saw my mother stumble down the steps, drop the knife, then pick it up again. "I'm going to get you some help, baby. I'm going. Oh, I swear to God, I didn't mean it," she cried, and started on her journey again.

I had never seen her like this before. After all she'd been through, I felt she had finally cracked. She'd finally lost her mind. It made me feel sick to my stomach. How was I supposed to rescue her, when she was running away from me? I was lost and confused. But, I had to keep going. I started to jump down four steps at a time in pursuit of her. Then it was five steps at a time. My bare feet continuously landed on dirty wrappers, forty-ounce bottles' brown paper bags, and all kinds of other paraphernalia. I was disgusted, and did all I could to not focus on the things that didn't matter, though the many syringes that were all over the hallway was a cause of concern for me. I did all I could to avoid them and managed to. My mother tried to jump down eight steps at a time, lost her footing, and wound up tumbling down the last three. Hit her head on the wall, and was knocked out cold. The bloody knife slid from her hands about five feet away from her. As soon as I made it to the bottom of the stairs where she was, the door to the ninth floor opened, and in walked one of the young door boys from my building.

"What the fuck?" he hollered, jumping back, and looking down at my mother's naked form.

I knelt beside her and lifted her so I could check the back of her head. "Mama, are you okay? Please be okay." Upon pulling my fingers from the back side of her afro, I came back with traces of blood all over them.

"Damn, ain't you old man Leon's daughter from upstairs? And, ain't this his wife?" the dude asked, looking both ways, then stepping back into the stairwell beside me. I could smell the scent of his cologne. It was a change of scent from the hallway that smelled like strong piss, and feces.

"Please don't call the police. My father was beating my mother up. She did everything she could to fight him off, but things just got blown out of proportion. Please, we just want to get out these projects. It's not safe for us here." I didn't know why I was rambling on the way I was, but I couldn't stop myself. The words just kept coming and coming. I think I was panicking, because I was sure my father was upstairs deceased and that if it was found out, my mother would be taken away from me and my sisters, leaving us all alone in a cold, cold world.

The man knelt down beside her and took his shirt off, placing it over her naked torso. "Yo, I don't get down wit Twelve like that, shorty. I ain't looking to turn y'all in. Besides, your old man is a rotten-ass nigga anyway for beating your mother like this. Let me help you get her up, come on." Instead of me helping him, he picked her up on his own, and held her in place. "Where we going?"

I stood up, still in panic mode. I knew anybody could come into the stairwell and spot us at any moment. The only option we had was to take her back to our place. From there, I would have to figure things out. I was so lost and disoriented that I was on the verge of becoming hysterical. "Bring her back to our place please and hurry up before somebody sees." I rushed up the stairs in front of them. Every so often, I would look over my shoulder to check and see how they were doing. The young dude kept on grunting every few steps, and whenever I asked to assist him, he seemed offended.

After what seemed like an eternity, we made it back to our floor, and as soon as I stepped onto the landing, I saw two, dirty-clothed, drug addicts running out our apartment with our DVD player and our microwave. They ran as fast as they could in the opposite direction. One of them hollered to the other, "Leon dead, blood. That nigga gone!"

"Hey! Hey!" I took off running behind them, but stopped after I made it halfway down the hall. I was more afraid of them than they were of getting caught by me and I was sure of that. So I stopped, breathing heavy and jogged back to our front door, rushed inside. "Ashley! Ashland! Are you guys okay?" One of the cardinal rules in the Red Hook Housing

Projects was that you were never supposed to leave your front door unlocked, because whenever you did, the addicts would just know about it. Their instincts were amazing. I was more worried about their knowledge of my father's state than anything else.

"Yeah, we're okay, big sis. Can we come out now, we're scared," Ashley hollered.

"Not yet! I'll be back there to get you two in a minute, I promise."

The dude carried my mother into the apartment and laid her on the couch. "Yo, I can tell she about to wake up. She doing a lot of groaning." He stopped and looked around at all the blood. "Dang, what the fuck happened in here?" There were bloody footprints all over the floor. His eyes bucked as he headed toward the kitchen. When he saw my father stretched out on his back, he stopped in place. "What, aw shit, that nigga Leon is laced." He jogged into the kitchen and knelt beside him. Pressed his finger to the right side of his neck, and shook his head. "Damn." Looked toward me, and grew concerned. "He gone, shorty."

I wiped a tear from my cheek. "I figured that. Can you please go? I have so many things I need to figure out. I gotta get my family out of here before the cops come. Ain't no telling what those dope addicts are about to do after they unload the items they stole from here." I saw my mother jerk in her sleep, her eyes opened wide, before she started to cry.

He came into the living room. "Look, I know I don't know you like that, but I ain't about to let y'all take the fall for this. If you want, I'll get rid of this punk-ass nigga for you. I don't fuck wit them women beaters, nah' mean. Far as I'm concerned, dude's bitch ass got everything he had coming to him," he snickered.

I cut daggers at him, as I sat on the couch beside my mother. "Can you watch your freaking mouth? Jesus. I have two little sisters down the hall. They don't need to hear that filthy language, they've heard enough." I pulled my mother into my embrace and rocked back and forth with her.

"Yo, I'm tryna help you out. You know how them rock heads get down in Red Hook. They'll sell their mother for the right price. I can see them at the station right now, trying to sell this murder. Whatever we gone do, we gotta hurry up. My apologies for my language, I ain't know no shorties was back there. You want me to go and check on 'em?" He stood up and looked down the hallway.

My mother sobbed into my shoulder. I continued to rock with her. My eyes scanned the living room. The rock heads had torn it apart and knocked over the entertainment system. Along with that, there were bloody footprints everywhere I looked. It was even starting to smell funny. "What is your name? Mine is Jade."

"Bentley, like the whip, and I already knew your name, shorty. I always said I couldn't understand how your ugly ass pops could make a daughter as bad as you, every time I saw him. That was a lil joke we had going."

I rolled my eyes. "How are you going to get rid of his body? How long would it take you?" I asked, starting to imagine the possibilities.

"No!" My mother head-butted me and broke off the couch, ran into the kitchen and lay on the floor with my father. "Ain't nobody about to touch him. Nobody! I'll kill all of you muthafuckas if you even try to touch my husband!" she screamed.

Bentley jumped back, held his hands shoulder length. "Look, shorty, I don't want no parts of this then. A, I don't wanna leave you in a sticky position like this, but your mother ain't giving me much of a choice. Just tell me what you wanna do and I'll help you as best I can." He stepped closer, frowned, and ran to me. "What happened to yo face?"

All while he'd been talking, my face had been in my hands. When I removed them, blood poured out of my nose and into my hands, from when my mother had head-butted me. I stood up, feeling dizzy. "Just go, I'll figure it out. I'll figure all of this out." Though these were the words I'd said, I didn't believe myself one bit. The truth was, I was terrified out of my mind. I knew if he didn't get my father out of there, we were going to be in some serious trouble.

He ran into the bathroom and came out with a bunch of tissue, grabbed me to his body, and forced me to place it over my nose. "Yo, hold yo head back, shorty. Hold it back or you gon wind up fainting."

I nodded. "Okay. Thank you." Not only was my nose bleeding, but my face was hurting so bad, I felt like crying. This had been a horrible day. I didn't know how it could get any worse.

Bentley walked into the kitchen and looked down on my crying mother. "Look, Miss Lady. I gotta get dude out of here, or you're going to jail. Now, I know you love him and all that, but you gotta be smart. You got three children to think about. Now watch out."

My mother laid with her back on my father. "Don't you put your filthy hands on my husband. If you touch him, I swear to God, I will kill you and everybody you love!" She turned over and hugged him. "Oh, I didn't mean to do this. What have I done? I'm so sorry, Leon, I'm so, so sorry."

Bentley stood there in shock. Shook his head and sighed out loud. "Yo, this a lost cause. I'm 'bout to get the fuck out of here, word up." He turned to me. "Jade, I wish I could help, but yo moms wiling, kid. Yo, it's in ya best interest to get the fuck out of here, before them boys show up. Once they do, all of ya asses are grass. Now, if you wanna bounce wit me, let's roll. I'll put you up until this situation is figured out. What's it gone be?"

I looked into the kitchen and saw my mother kissing all over my father's face. The floor was a blood bath. It was starting to freak me out more and more by the second. "I-I-I got my sisters in the other room. I can't leave them behind. Then, I don't know you. Why should I trust you?" I began to shake. Felt like things were about to get a lot worse. My vision became cloudy. The blood coming out of my nostrils had saturated the tissue already. I was having a hard time of standing up.

He waved me off. "You right, you don't know me, but common sense a' tell you, you gotta get up out of here real fast. Yo pops is gone. That nigga ain't never coming back. Word up. And yo mother? Shorty seem like she's out of her mind. My word, queen, you need to be on the move wit yo sisters back there. This the last time I'ma ask you, you wanna roll out wit me or what?"

I was starting to panic again. My mother was unchanged, her sobs were louder than before, and now she'd managed to flip my father on top of her. It looked ridiculous. I was on the verge of telling Bentley to give me a second so I could go and get my sisters, but he lost his patience.

"Man, fuck this. I'm out of here." He waved me off and ran out the door.

As soon as he did, I fell to my knees, and started to bawl. I didn't know what to do. The rats seemed to come out of their hiding places throughout the apartment. They circled around my parents, licking up the spattered blood. Down the hall I could hear my sisters crying, asking why. That broke my heart because I didn't know what to tell them, or how I was going to rescue them. It was all too much too soon. I got woozy, then felt dizzier then I ever had before. The next thing I knew, my body went weak and my eyes crossed, then I passed out.

* * *

When I woke up, Bentley was running down the hallway with me in his arms. My head bounced up and down on my neck. My vision was extremely blurry, and my consciousness took its time coming full surface. But, as soon as it did, I perked up in his arms. "Ashley! Ashland! My sisters! Where are you taking me? Let me down!" I snapped, beating at his shoulders to be released immediately.

He kept running. "Shorty, chill. Twelve all over your crib right now. They done already snatched ya moms. It ain't safe." He got outside an apartment door, twisted the knob and it opened. Entered it backwards with me still in his arms and once inside, he laid me on the couch.

I bounced right up and made a run for the door. "I gotta get up there before they take my sisters. I can't let them wind up in foster care!" I felt dizzy as soon as I stood up. Staggered on my feet and fell to the carpet, disoriented.

Bentley came and scooped me as if I was light as a feather. Carried me back to the couch and sat me on it slowly. "Look, Jade, I need you to chill. I know yo peoples up there, but I'm telling you, it's swarming with the Jakes right now. They ain't about to give you them lil girls. The only thing they gon do is lock you up and that ain't cool, because you ain't ice yo old man, ya moms did. I heard her admit that over and over. But, she out of her mind right now, so who knows what she's saying? Why don't you just chill here until the heat dies down, then we'll go checking around the building to see what's good." He disappeared into the kitchen, and came back out with an ice bag, as if he had it on standby. Handed it to me and gave me a look of concern.

My head was pounding, both on the inside, and on the outside. I was still a bit dizzy, and borderline nauseous. I sat up as best I could. "Bentley, you don't understand. I am all my sisters have if the police are going to arrest my mother. I know they can't take them into a cell with her, so where will they go. I simply must get up. I have to." I sat all the way up and got so dizzy, I had to close my eyes immediately. There was a steady throbbing behind my eyes. The pain was so evident, it brought me to tears.

He knelt beside me and took the ice bag out of my hand. Placed it against my forehead and with gentle force, led me backward. My head wound up on one of his throw pillows. His generosity was throwing me for a loop. My father had shown me with his actions the male species was not to be trusted. They were dangerous, selfish, and abusive in all of its forms. I couldn't understand what this man was up to, but I didn't trust him in the least bit. I had to muster up the strength, so I could get up and find my sisters. God only knows what would happen to them.

"Look, Jade, you need to fall back for a little while. I'ma hit up the building and see what's really good wit Twelve. Sniff around to see what the word is, if shit looking a lil dangerous, then I'ma come back and tell you. But honest to God, ma, it ain't safe out there right now." He held the ice pack to my forehead and looked into my brown eyes with his own. "I'm not gon hurt you. I know you been through a lot, but please just trust me right now." His breath smelled like spearmint gum. His cologne was just a bit too strong for me. Too masculine, it made me think about my father. I needed to get out of his house. The longer I stayed, the more I worried about my sisters, and his true intentions of bringing me to his place. I knew for a fact that dope boys didn't care about women, and he was most definitely that. I would tell him what he wanted to hear, so I could bounce once he left. Yeah, that was my only hope.

I nodded my head. "Okay, Bentley. Why don't you go and check the scene, and I'll stay here until I feel better. That way, you can relay back to me what's being said, and where they may be taking my sisters. I'd really appreciate it if you did." My voice was strained, and my heart was racing so fast that I could barely breathe. I closed my eyes, and both Ashley and Ashland's faces appeared. It made me even sadder.

He smiled briefly. His handsome face lit up. I noticed he had two deep dimples, one on each jaw. His eye brows were thick, almost too thick. His lips full and beautiful shade of brown. There was a prominent mole on the left side of his cheek. He wore his beard cut into a goatee, expertly trimmed and cut. There were tattoos all over his arms, and one on the right side of his neck. He was a thug in every sense of the word. I had to break free of his captivity.

"Yo, that sound like a plan, goddess. I'ma go out here and see what's good. You just lean back and I'll return in no more than thirty minutes. My word is bond." He ran into the back room. I could hear him opening and closing what sounded like dresser drawers. Then, he was back in the living room. The butt of his gun poked at his shirt in the back. "In a minute, shorty, just chill. If you need anything, feel free to do you." He opened the door. "Oh, and if a slightly older man come before I get back and he's rocking a mechanic's uniform, that's my pops. He cool. I'm sending him a quick text to let him know a snapshot of what's what, just in case though. Get you some rest." He opened and closed the door. I could hear him lock it from the outside. I waited five minutes to make sure that he was gone, and jumped up. I had to find my sisters.

Chapter 4

Bentley

"Yo, so when you got back, you telling me that shorty was just gone, kid?" Santana asked, poppin' two Xans and chasing them with a pink Sprite. He let his seat back, and looked over at me. Tried to hand me the Sprite, but I pushed his hand away. He shrugged his shoulders and turned the bottle back up.

"Yeah, Dunn, ma left the door wide open and everything. One of them rock heads coulda stole everything me and my pops had. Yo, that's the last time I try and help anybody, word up." I was still reeling on the situation that had taken place almost two weeks ago, with Jade and her peoples. Couldn't believe she had not taken heed to my advice. After snooping around the building, I found out her mother had been taken in for the murder of her father, and the twin girls had been snatched by Child Protective Services. I broke my neck to get back to my apartment so I could inform Jade, only to find it empty, and the front door slightly ajar. That had been fifteen days ago and still there had been no sign of Jade. There was still a heavy police presence because of the incident, and they were questioning people in regards to her whereabouts. Rumor had it that her mother was blaming the murder on her. At least, that's how it was broadcast on the news. But, I didn't know for sure.

Santana scratched his forehead under his red bandana. "Kid, you ain't know that bitch or her peoples like that, anyway. Ain't no way the god woulda been trying to assist no broad wit a body. These Yankees giving niggas the needle for shit like that. Besides, we got too much other shit on our plate anyway." He flipped a switch, and the hard top to the drop disconnected from the top of the windshield, and moved backward until it disappeared in the trunk of the Beamer. The seats were all white, and leather. The BMW was newly released and fresh off the showroom for only four days prior. It still had that new car smell.

"I stumbled upon her moms in a fucked-up position, god. Yo, goddess was naked and everything. Battered and beaten, with blood all over her. Then, Jade looked just as bad. I had to step in. Besides, Jade used to go to Malcolm X with me. So, I'm familiar with her, I just ain't know her like that. That's all." I'd seen her often at school when I did attend the year before, and the years before then and I always thought she was one of the baddest bitches in the building. But, I never came at her or nothing like that. Then once I found out she was Leon's daughter, whole relation through me off a lil bit. That nigga, Leon, was super gross to me. He had a habit of screwing the crack head prostitutes in the hallways, or the stairwells as if it was the most natural thing in the world. I found that shit disgusting. Once I found out he and Jade were kin, every time I saw her after that, I saw his features and that fucked up the physical attraction I had to her. So, before I knew it, she was old news and I started jocking the second baddest bitch at school named Keri. She was Black and Puerto Rican, with long curly hair, bangin' body, and jazzy as a muthafucka, just like I liked my women. On top of that, she was about her money.

"Yeah well, I still wouldn't have helped. Her and that ol broad would have been on their own if I had anything to say about it. You know the streets barking and they saying shorty is the one that laced her pops, that her mother caught her in the act of stabbing Leon up. They gon give her ass the needle for that when they catch her, B, word up." Santana made a right turn at the light, and turned in his system. I could hear

Lil Wayne's *Tha Carter V* coming out of the speakers. He was spitting about his hittas.

I got irritated and mugged Santana. That nigga was always getting his facts from the streets, and rarely ever was the streets right. I knew for a fact Jade had not iced her old man. I wondered where she was hiding. A part of me hoped she was safe. "Anyway, bruh, what's on the agenda for the day?" I wanted to switch the conversation and get on something else. The subject of Jade and her family was getting me vexed for some reason.

"I'm 'bout to roll through Harlem and get up wit my mans about this drop off. He gon hit me for this whip I'm rolling, then me and you gon go and snatch up something fresh that's worth the fifty-fifty split, nah mean?" He sucked his teeth, and turned his Sprite up again. Downing it so fast that the bottle folded inward before he replaced it in the console of the BMW.

Flipping cars was one of our hustles. Santana and I were geniuses when it came to stealing cars, and bussing them down for profit. In fact, the car game is how me and Santana had gotten cool, and became best friends. Back in the day when we were both just eleven years old, we had a small crew that ran around Brooklyn stealing cars, just for the hell of it. Our crews would compete with each other to see which crew could come up with the fastest, most expensive, most exclusive cars. We'd meet in back of the old can place four blocks down from the Red Hook Houses, and have project bitches judge which crew was riding the flyest. Whoever lost had to hand over their cars, and the crew that won would be left with the cars and the girls. I hated to lose, and had only lost once.

But, one day, Santana came to me and told me he had some boss nigga out in Harlem that ran a chop shop. Said he

would give us a gee for each car we brought them, long as the cars were foreign, or made overseas. I jumped down with him that day, and that had been our hustle ever since then. One day, I wanted to own my own car lot though. I wanted to own a car lot that would have top notch whips for the low. That way, almost everybody from the projects could cop one, and for the ones that couldn't afford to, I would meet them halfway.

"Aiight, that's cool, but whatever you finna get, I gotta have half of that. My pockets empty right now and rent is due tomorrow. I gotta have my end. My pops already handled all the rest of the bills, so I at least gotta do this."

Santana nodded. "What's mine is yours, god, you already know that. Although I gotta say, if you'd keep yo dick out of yo old man's bitch, maybe you'd be able to focus on yo hustle. Blood gon snap if he ever find out you been piping his wife," he snickered. "Damn, you an animal. She got some good ass pussy too, don't she?" He got on the highway, and stepped on the accelerator.

That was one of Santana's downfalls. Sometimes he was too nosey for his own good. I didn't like nobody being in my business. I didn't give a fuck how cool we were. "Yo, stay in yo lane son. Word up. Nigga, I swear I wish you would have never caught me smashing shorty last month. I still don't know how I left my keys in your car. Worst mistake I ever made." Because I had left my keys in Santana's whip, that gave him leeway to show up unannounced to return them. Well, it just so happened on that night, me and Asia were doing our thing in my pops' bed. I'd been wearing that ass out from the back, talking all nasty to her and shit when Santana barged in the room. On that day, I was thankful it had been him and not my father, but now I wasn't so sure. He'd found a way to bring up me and Asia's forbidden relationship every single day, since he first discovered it. I was sure he had a thing for her fine ass, but I never asked. My irritation always got the better of me.

He laughed. "Nigga, I know that pussy bet not be getting you all whipped and shit. That's your father's wife. Damn. That bitch trifling anyway, fucking her son-in-law. Shoulda seen that coming. Why they don't live together now that they married? That shit odd."

I shrugged my shoulders. "Don't know and don't care. Ain't my bidness, and ain't yours either. Let's buss this move and get on something new. I can see you tryna make me go there wit yo yellow ass today, word up. I ain't gon bite the apple though." I felt myself getting heated.

He laughed. "Yeah, I'm just fucking wit you. I know you always get vexed when we get to talking about shorty ass, so I just wanted to give you a hard time. That's my bad, Blood, I'ma fall back." He pulled a Dutch out of the ashtray, and handed it to me. "Spark that and float away, my nigga. The sun is shining. Before the day is out, you should have at least five gees in your pocket. We gon snatch up a few bitches to kick back wit and fuck up a storm, you know how we do." He turned up *Tha Carter V*, and we both got to nodding our heads while Wayne spit through the speakers.

***

That day, I made a quick five bands wit Santana before Asia hit up my phone, saying she needed my help back at the projects immediately. She wouldn't tell me what the issue was, and because Santana had to make a trip out to D.C. and I didn't want to accompany him, I headed back to the projects as soon as I could. When I got in the building, I ran up the stairs and all the way to the apartment, by the time I got there, I was out of breath. The hallway was filthy. There was trash all over it, and big rats roamed up and down. There was a heavy aroma of piss and cigarette smoke. I beat on her door, and continued to watch the rodents scurry along the edge of the walls, sniffing and screeching. It gave me the heebie-jeebies.

I could hear the sounds of Ella Mai crooning from the speakers inside her apartment. I beat on the door again, confused and a bit worried that somethin' bad had happened. She opened the door a minute later, dressed in a short, pink silk Victoria's Secret robe. Most of her thick thighs were exposed. The scent of her perfume drifted into the hallway. She wore bright red lipstick on her juicy lips. They appeared to be coated with a thick layer of gloss. "Hey, lil daddy, look what I got for you." She came from behind her back with a small knot of money. I peeped that there was a fifty onto of the knot. I didn't know how much it was, but before I left her crib, I was dead set on having every bit of it.

I frowned and stormed past her, after seeing she'd used the emergency ploy to get me to come to her crib. It hadn't been the first time, and I was sure it wouldn't be the last. I need to play my role. Needed to act like I was pissed off, so I could get that paper she was flashing in front of me. "Bitch, I know you text me, talking about a fucking emergency. I rush my dumb ass all the way over here worried about you, then when I got here, you flashing this short-ass knot in my face. Yo, tell me that ain't what's good." I mugged her with mounting anger, and flared my nostrils.

She closed the door. "Baby, please don't be angry at me. I just knew you were out in those streets and probably laid up with some bitch. I knew if I didn't say it was an emergency, you would have probably not come, when I needed you. I need you so, so bad. Look." She placed her back against the door, and slowly raised the hem to her silk robe, lifted it high enough to expose her bald pussy. It was freshly shaven. The lips were puffy, and smushed into one another, they looked so delectable. She slid a finger through them before sucking it into her mouth.

I had to stay the course. I needed that bread in her hand. "Yo, fuck that pussy. You know how much money I'm losing right now? Yo, I'll fuck wit you at another time." I headed for the door, acting like I was about to bounce, when in actuality, the sight of that bald pussy had me feening for a shot of her.

She stayed in front of the door. "Look, baby. This is eight fifty right here. I know it ain't much, but it's yours. Just stay wit me for a few hours. I feel so alone right now." She placed her hands together in prayer fashion. "Please, lil daddy. I need you." She poked out her bottom lip.

I looked up from head to toe. The way the robe was made, I could see through it. Her dark brown areolas were visible and the nipples erect. She opened her lips far enough for me to see her inner pink. Her clit popped out at the top of her hood. She trapped it between the fingers on her right hand.

I frowned, and held out my hand. My dick began to rise in my pants. "Let me get that."

She handed it to me, and stepped into my face. Kissed my lips, then sucked on them hard. "I been thinking about you all day, Bentley. Driving myself crazy over wondering if you were laid up with some other bitch. I don't know if I can handle that no more. Every time we get together, I feel myself falling more and more for you emotionally. This shit is dangerous." She kissed my neck and dropped to her knees, unbuckling my belt.

"Shorty, why you marry my pops if all you gon do is think about his son all day? That don't make no sense." I slid the money into my back pocket, before she dropped my pants to my ankles.

She looked up and grabbed ahold of my pipe, stroking it up and down. "You can't help who you fall for. I mean, I love yo daddy, but you just do something to me I can't explain. You give me butterflies and he don't. Ugh, I been waiting to taste this all day." She sucked me into her mouth, and moaned around the head. "Mmmm." Her eyes closed, a slight smile cast upon her face.

I grabbed her by the hair and yanked her off me. "Then, what the fuck you marry him for, huh? Why you make him cheat on my mother? You know she doing that dope because of you and him? Huh?" I grabbed a handful of her hair and yanked on it harder. She yelped and that encouraged me to hurt her further. The sight of my mother played across my mind's eye. The last time I had seen her, she'd been with a group of rock heads in the boiler room of the projects, getting high as a kite. The sight broke my heart.

Asia reached and took my piece into her small hand and squeezed it. "Lil daddy, you know I didn't even know your mother when me and Lincoln got to messing around. He made it seem as if he and your mother were nothing more than friends. You can't blame that on me. Please, baby. You know I would have never set out to hurt anybody. Now, please give me some." She started to pull away from the hold I had on her hair, trying her best to wrap her lips back around my piece. It looked almost comical, and it was also a turn-on. I couldn't help hiding my arousal. Her tongue swiped at it.

That sent a chill down my spine. As much as I hated to admit it, Asia had a sexual hold on me. She'd introduced me to so many things sexually that I felt woke. My body called out for her almost as much as hers did for me. I hated that reality. I wrapped my fingers a bit tighter, and guided myself into her mouth. It got hot, and swampy. She tightened her lips and started to go right to work on me, sucking loudly, covering it with spit, and moaning the whole time. All of the noise was driving me crazy.

"Damn, shorty, slow down. Slow down. Shit."

She got to pumping me up and down real fast. Got it super wet, then removed her hands from it and really got to taming me. I backed up into the wall and curled my toes, whimpering like a bitch in heat. Asia's head game was top-notch. She popped me out of her mouth, and looked up at me. "Feel good, baby. Huh? You almost ready to fuck me?" She continued to stroke me.

I was out of breath and on the verge of spilling. I looked down at her through squinted eyes. "Bitch, stop playin' wit me. Finish what you started. Put my shit back in yo mouth. Hurry up." Once again, I tightened my fingers in the strands of her hair.

"Un. Nall, I want you to taste me now. Get me to where you are so we can do our thing, Bentley. You know I'll hit you off right. I always do." She slid her hand under her stomach and separated her sex lips. Slid them into herself, then wiped them on my lips. "Taste me."

My tongue shot out on its own accord, licking at her fingers, and tasting her forbidden salty juices. The taste was savory. Made goose bumps appear on my arms. I released her hair. Picked her up and sat her on the kitchen table, after moving a box of pizza out of the way. Yanked her robe all the way up to her stomach and pulled up a chair, sitting in it. "Wrap them thick ass thighs around my face. Come on."

She did just that. Lined her cat up with my mouth and laid back in the table, humping her hips up and down, riding my tongue. "Un. Un. Un. Oh. Yes, baby. Yes. Damn, Bentley. I love you so much." She grabbed the back of my head and forced me further into her gap.

I held my tongue out and moved my head from side to side. Sucked on her kitty lips, pulled on them, then focused strictly on her clit, treated it like a nipple. Applied suction, and twirled my tongue around it over and over, swallowing the juices that leaked from her hole. I gripped her big booty that sat bare on the table and feasted like a savage, loving her taste, intoxicated by the earthly scent of her pussy.

"Bentley, eat that thang, baby. Eat that thang. Dis why I'm so obsessed wit yo ass. Uh-shit! Here I go. Here I gooooooooooo!" She humped into my face faster and faster, cumming hard. Her thighs were crossed around my neck. After she came, she opened them wide. I witnessed her juices leaking out of her and sliding from her inner thigh, down to the table.

I licked all over her. Sucked her inner thighs, then bit both, before standing up. Yanked her to me and lined myself up. Placed an ankle on each shoulder, and slammed forward with no mercy.

She shrieked and opened her mouth wide. "Wait, baby. Let's go in the bedroom, just in case yo daddy pop up out the blue. We can't let him catch us like this."

"Shut up, bitch, and give me this shit." I cocked back, and slammed into her tight fit again. Then I got to long stroking her, watching her titties spill out of her robe. The nipples were stuck straight out. The baby bump was slightly visible from the angle. Her cat felt tighter than usual.

52

Life of Sin

Bam. Bam. Bam. Tkk. Tkk. Tkk.
Were the sounds our skin made as they crashed into each other. The table moved backward inch by inch. The box of pizza fell from it and hit the floor, and I kept right on going. Licking all over her right ankle that was closest to my face, she guided it so her big toe wound up in my mouth. I sucked it like a thumb.

Her hands roamed all over my back. "Damn, Bentley. Damn, baby. Uh shit, baby. You're killing me. You killing me. Bentley!" She dug her nails into my back and pulled.

I thrust faster and pounded harder, giving her my all. Held onto her big thighs and dug as far into her as I could, before splashing her walls with my seed again and again. It felt so good that my knees got weak and buckled me. I pulled out and had to gather myself. I staggered backward into the refrigerator. My piece was throbbing in the air, our juices dripping from it. I took breaths to get some oxygen to flow to my brain.

She hopped off the table, and turned around with her ass facing me. Her hand slid between her thighs again. "Hit this from the back, Bentley. I'm so close, baby. I'm so, so close." I watched her open her lips to entice me.

I bounced from the refrigerator and got behind her, smacked that juicy booty twice, nice and hard. Then I ran my head up and down her slit, before pushing inside and going to work, smacking that ass in between strokes. That drove her up the wall, in less than five minutes she came, pushing back into me, screaming at the top of her lungs. We heard the key jiggling in the lock of her front door, and scrambled to break apart from each other, but before I could pull my pants up, the door flew open and my father rushed in with a .45 in his hand, and a bewildered look spread across his dark face.

"I should have known you and this tricking bitch was doing this behind my back! Every instinct in my bones told me y'all was!" He cocked the hammer. "But, that's okay, 'cause you two muthafuckas are about to die."

I slid my pants up, and backed away. "Yo, Pop, it ain't what you thinking. Me and Asia ain't mean to hurt you, it just happened this one time," I lied, backing away from him, and trying to think of my next move.

My old man wasn't known for being a killer, but at the same time, I knew he was crazy about Asia. He'd expressed that to me on more than one occasion. To be honest, I think that fact is what made her pussy so good to me. In a way, I felt like every time I fucked her, I was hurting my father the same way he'd hurt my mother by cheating on her with Asia. I ain't feel no sympathy. I just wasn't trying to get shot over his bitch's pussy. She wasn't worth all that to me.

Asia hopped off of the table. "Baby, can you listen to me for a second? Please." She pulled her robe down, then tied the sash around it again. Her left breast hung out of it, before she tucked it in and blushed. Held her hands out, walking toward my father. "Baby, I've been lonely. You've been working way too much, and I needed to be physically taken care of. I told you I would never sleep with another man outside of you, and I didn't. Bentley is your blood. Y'all are one and the same.

I shot a glance at this bitch and almost snapped my neck. Out of all of the excuses she could've come up with, she'd chosen one so morose. I looked into my father's dark face to see if he was buying any of the bullshit she was selling.

He leveled the gun at her. "Bitch, you're lower than a basement. Out of all of the men in the world to go behind my back with, you choose to do it with my son. I wish I would have never gotten your dumb ass pregnant." He furrowed his eyebrows, and pressed the gun to her forehead. "Don't you know I love you? Huh?"

I tried to slowly slide my way out of the kitchen with my hands raised. As far as I was concerned, this was between them. I couldn't see myself fucking wit her on that level no more. I could still taste her pussy on my tongue. I couldn't help noticing that. Just as I was about to ease out of the kitchen, my father jumped back and aimed his gun at me, stopping me in my tracks.

"Where the fuck you think you going, turn-coat? You gon stab a knife in my back and think you about to walk away unscathed? You got another thang coming. I can't believe you'd do me like this." His eyes were bloodshot, watery. I couldn't look directly at him. Emotionally, the sight of him was affecting me negatively.

"So, what you gon do, Lincoln? You gon kill us? Huh? You gon kill us for playing around a lil bit, when you know damn well you ain't been on your game lately? Every time I've come to you for you to take care of my physical needs, you've done nothing but pushed me to the side. I've been trying every single day for the last two weeks. Haven't I?" she said in a calm manner.

He shook his head. "I been tired, Asia. I work in that body shop twelve hours every single day at minimum. Sometimes sixteen hours straight. When I get home, all I want to do is rest. I ain't got the energy to go there wit you. I wish I did, but I just don't." He blinked, and a tear fell from each eye. He wiped them away, and kept the gun trained on me.

"Then what was I supposed to do, big daddy? Did you want me to go out in the street and find some other man to handle my needs? Is that what you would have preferred?"

T.J. & Jelissa

The scent of our sex session was heavy in the air. It didn't help that her apartment was so hot. She needed to open a window a somethin'. I backed away again. "Pop stop pointing that gun at me. Yo, I ain't mean to hurt you. I know you ain't 'bout to shoot me over no female. Come on now. I'm your kid."

He raised the gun so it was aimed right at my face. "Far as I'm concerned, you just another nigga that wanna fuck my wife and take her away from me. You'sa trifling ass nigga. Living off me. Making me pay all of the bills while you rip and run the streets, and fuck my wife behind my back. Meanwhile, I'm bussing my ass to provide for a bitch that can't even respect herself enough to not fuck her own stepson, while her husband is at work slaving. Both of you muthafuckas deserve a bullet. This bitch just lucky she got my baby growing inside of her, or I'd light her up like a Christmas tree. But you, you I can shoot with no problem, you'd be one less burden of mine." He mugged me and turned the gun sideways.

I swallowed and nodded my head. "That's how you really feel, huh?"

"That's just how I feel, so what you got to say about that?" he asked, stepping forward a foot closer to me.

Asia backed away and sank to the floor in front of the stove, with her knees to her chest, pussy on full display. I was sure she wasn't aware of it. "We're sorry, Lincoln. Please don't hurt your son. We didn't mean to do what we did. I just need it so much, now that I'm pregnant."

I waved her off. "Nall, bitch, don't speak for me." Looked directly into my father's eyes. "I don't apologize for fucking her. Nall, Pa, why should I? That pregnant pussy is fye. Plus, she nice and tight, I can tell you ain't been putting no work in, because her gates are too close together."

Asia stood up. "Bentley, please don't provoke him. Lincoln, he just angry, baby. Please, let's just talk about this like adults." She placed four fingers to her teeth and got to chewing on them, nervously.

"Nall, if he gone pop me, then he gon know what's really good." I looked back into his eyes. "You ain't have no sympathy when you was cheating on my mother wit this bitch, and I ain't got no sympathy for making this bitch cheat on you wit me. It's the circle of betrayal, get over it. You got my moms out here smoking dope, and stressing because of how you treated her, and now you wanna run and get ya gun when she do yo ass the same way you did somebody else. Cry me a fucking river, nigga, you gon shot me then do it. Fuck you waiting on?"

Tears dropped out of his eyes. He took a deep breath, closed his lids, and started to squeeze on the trigger over and over. Bit into his bottom lip, and opened his eyes wide to see what the problem was. By the time he was able to discover he had to flip it off safety, I watched him adjust it, then I rushed him and smacked the gun out of his hand. It fell to the floor and went off.

Boom.

Asia flew backward into the pantry screaming at the top of her lungs. "Awww! I'm hit! Awww, I'm hit! Oh, it hurts so bad! It hurts so bad!"

Me and my father wrestled on the floor. He was cock-strong. Much stronger than me, but I fought as if my life depended on it. And by the way he was grunting and trying to overpower me, it probably was. He slammed his elbow into the side of my face, and head-butted me as hard as he could, busting my nose. The back of my head crashed into the floor, but I couldn't feel the pain, my adrenalin was coursing through me on flight for life mode. I brought my knee upward and directly into his sack.

Wham!

His eyes got bucked, he hollered out loud and fell off me holding himself. "Ah, you son of a bitch. I'ma kill you. I swear I'ma kill you," he promised.

I stood up with blood pouring out of my nose. Wiped it away. I thought about kicking him in the ribs as hard as I could, but the man in me wouldn't allow it. Even though we were in a fight, he was still my father and because he was, I couldn't cause him bodily harm like that. Felt like I had screwed him over enough by smashing his pregnant wife on a regular basis behind his back. So, I stood over him shaking in anger. Now my blood ran over my lips. "Yo, I was bogus, Pop. I shouldn't have done what I did, but you shouldn't have did what you did to my mother either."

Asia stumbled out of the pantry, holding her shoulder. "I'm shot. I'm fucking shot. Y'all can talk about this shit later." She fell to her knees, and then onto her chest, before curling into a ball on her side, shaking.

"You going to jail, Bentley. As soon as I get up, I'm calling the police. You shot her. You betta run. You betta run long and don't stop until you're way out of New York City. If the police don't catch you, then I will. You gon pay for this," my father grumbled, holding his privates. His dark-skinned face had turned a reddish brown.

"You know what, Pop, you ain't nothin but a pussy. Now you calling Twelve. My word, I ain't got no respect for a nigga like you. For as long as you wit that bitch, she gon be feening for this dick, 'cause you don't measure up. If I had my way, I'd—"

There was an intense banging on the door.

Bomp. Bomp. Bomp.

Life of Sin

"Open up! New York City Police Department, we've been given permission to search the premises by the Housing Authority. There's been reports of shots fired from this residence. Open up or we'll be forced to knock the door down."

T.J. & Jelissa

Chapter 5

Jade

"Please, please, please don't let it rain again." I closed my eyes and clasped my fingers together, begging the heavens. I didn't think I could take another night of thunderstorms and cold winds. The abandoned aluminum warehouse was cold enough and it was so old, the ceilings were leaking.

In addition to that, every time it rained, countless drug addicts and homeless people chose to seek refuge on the premises. This terrified me, because I was always worried about one of the men spotting me, and being so hyped up on drugs, they'd try doing only God knows what to me. I was alone, defenseless, and on the run for my life. The only clothes I owned were the one set I had on. They were filthy, reeked of a foul odor, and the knees in the jeans had already started to tear. The shoes were wet on the inside from yesterday's storm, and before I ran away from him, I'd only managed to grab a blouse from Bentley's father's house, along with a red bomber jacket. But, I thank God I was smart enough to grab that jacket, it was the only thing that had kept me warm at night.

I waited until the employees from the barbecue joint opened the back door to the establishment, came into the alley and threw the night's garbage into the big dumpster, before slamming the door back. The lightning sparked across the sky. Thunder roared like an angry lion, helping me to understand what I'd be up against in a matter of minutes. I had to act fast. I looked both ways, up and down the alley. It was empty, and dark. About a block down, I could see cars going past every now and again. The lightning flashed again, and then the rain broke through the clouds as if a pipe had burst. The bomber jacket was without a hood, so it left me vulnerable to the elements of Mother Nature, but I was strong. I would brave them. I had no other choice. This was the life of a person on the run, the life of the desolate.

I broke as fast as I could to the dumpster and hoisted myself up. Jumped inside of it and located the fresh bag of garbage the barbecue joint had tossed out. Picked it up and tried to sniff out the food through the plastic, but was unsuccessful. I was starving and had not eaten in almost twenty-four hours. I felt weak and just a bit disoriented. I ripped open the plastic just enough to see the contents, by using the alley light that flickered off and on. There was a heavy scent of barbecued meat that rushed my nostrils. I didn't hesitate. Dug my hand into the bag and gripped what felt like a whole baby back rib. Pulled it out, and bit into it. Ripped the meat from the bone, and chewed it with my eyes closed. It was so good, I felt like crying. Before I could swallow it all the way, I was ripping more from the bone like a hungry lioness. The sauce coated my cheeks. I was smacking loud, like I didn't have any home training.

The rain started to come down even harder. The thunder rumbled angrily. I finished the whole rib, dug into the bag and grabbed another one, and ripped it to shreds as well. After the completion of that one, I separated the food contents from the trash inside the bag. Then, I looked to jump out of the dumpster. I tied the bag in a knot and tossed it over, then slowly climbed out of it. Everything was slippery, so I had to be as careful as possible, because I was already a bit of a klutz. So I took my time, and made it safely to the ground. Picked up the bag, and pulled my coat over my head. Lightning flashed and as it lit up the sky, it illuminated two distant figures in the alley. I couldn't tell whether they were male or female, until one of them spoke up.

"Hey! Bitch, you bet not be taking our food. If so, hand it over!" a feminine voice shouted about fifty feet away from me.

I backed up and picked up the bag that I'd dropped. Three more figures had suddenly come from nowhere. "Hey, it's first come, first serve here. I don't owe you nothing." I sounded tougher than I felt. I could feel the meat from the ribs stuck in my teeth. I looked toward the woman and tried to see if she'd been walking with a man or a woman. The three figures in the other direction were huge, and definitely looked masculine. I couldn't go their way, so the odds were against me.

The woman had on a beige jacket, with a black hood. She looked real skinny. Her boots were bright red like my jacket. The figure behind her looked about her size. I concluded that she was also female. At least, I hoped I was right because I was going through them, and I wasn't giving up my food. I was willing to fight all five of them before that happened. Hunger pains weren't a joke, and it really sucked for me because I couldn't go out and hunt in the daytime for food because there was a warrant for my arrest. I'd made the front page of the newspaper. I was being looked at as a person of interest in my father's murder.

Two days after my mother's arrest, and my sister's abduction by the City of New York's Child Protective Services, I'd read all the details in a paper left behind in the Walmart bathroom I'd used. The article had ripped my heart down the middle. According to it, my mother was saying that my father and I had gotten into a big argument about me coming in the house way after my curfew. That he'd slapped me around a few times, before I waited until he turned his back and stabbed him to death. She said she'd witnessed it all, and that directly after his murder, she and I had gotten into a big fight. I'd beaten her senseless, then ran away from home. It was crazy.

The three figures got closer. "Say, baby, I'm sure it's enough for all of us to share. How about this, you share the food and I'll share this boy wit you. I got a taste that a knock yo socks off, lil mama, trust that," said one of the male figures. He held out an aluminum foil package that reflected the alley light.

I got ready to run. "Y'all stay away from me. I don't do that shit. I was just hungry. Stay away!" I took off running in the direction of the two women. They closed the narrow path to the alley and looked as if they were ready to tackle me to the ground. I was terrified to say the least, looked over my shoulder and saw the three men chasing me as well. This really spooked me. The water in the alley splashed up as I ran as fast as I could. When I got to the two women, I took the bag of food and swung it as hard as I could into the woman's face that tried to bear hug me. She hollered and fell backward. I pushed her ass and kept on running, looking over my shoulder to see the men gaining on me. "Stay away. Stay away! Please stay away." I tried my best to pick up speed. The rain appeared to be working against me. It was pouring so bad that I couldn't really see in front of me. My coat felt heavy, and I felt like I was running in slow motion. I couldn't breathe. "Please."

One of them grabbed my jacket and tried to pull me. This freaked me all the way out. "Get over here, bitch. I want some of that fresh pussy. C'mere!"

I turned around and slammed the bag in his face, and went to kick him in the nuts like my mother had taught me.

Life of Sin

The foot landed harder, dropped him. He grabbed the bag and fell to the concrete wit it. I took off running again.

"C'mere, bitch!" called another predator. When I looked over my shoulder, I saw three people chasing me now and gaining ground.

I knew I didn't have much more distance in me. My legs felt like jelly. My lungs were burning, over worked, and ready to quit on me. One of the men grabbed me around the waist and tackled me to the ground. We landed in a puddle of muddy water. The splash sent it all over my face, even into my mouth. "Yeah, I got that ass now. Ooo, and she feel so shapely. Jack-muthafucking-pot!" He straddled me.

I brought my knee up and into his sack as hard as I could, crunching his family jewels. He rolled right off of me. I struggled to get up and was tackled again, this time by a female. She slapped me across the face and tried to choke me, her nails digging into the skin of my neck.

"Who do you think you are? Who do you think you are, bitch?" Her hood fell backward, leaving me with the sight of her ugly, dark-skinned, sunken face. Her grip was so tight, I couldn't pry it loose. She was starting to choke me and there was nothing I could do about it. I lay there gagging.

Another figure came and stood over her. The first woman I'd knocked to the ground. Her clothes and jacket were caked with mud, along with her pretty, yet sunken face. Even in the position I was in, her beauty was noticeable. She stood looking down on me for a short moment. "Cathy, that's enough. You're killing her. That's somebody's baby. Stop."

I lay there, struggling to breathe, no longer putting up a fight. The rain splashed into my face. *So, this is how I'm going to go out*, I thought, *choked out by a heroin addict in the middle of an alley in East New York*. What a life.

"She ain't my baby. This ho gotta go. Rest in hell, bitch!"
She choked me harder and harder. Then, her entire crew was
standing around, witnessing my murder.

The pretty-faced woman tried to pry her arms apart. "Get
off of her. That's a baby!" She brought her hand backward,
then forward with blazing speed, smacking her so hard that
she fell halfway off of me, but her hands were still around
my neck.

One of the men grabbed her, and slung her into another
dumpster. He moved Cathy out of the way and straddled me,
ripped the bomber jacket down the middle, and then my
blouse, baring my breasts. His filthy hands pawed all over
them. "Yeah bitch, 'bout to have us some tropical sex.
Mmm-hmmm, it ain't nothing like it either." I felt his
knuckles pressed against my stomach, then his fingers
worked on the buttons to my jeans.

The air came back into my lungs. I kicked my legs wild-
ly. "No! No! Please! Help me! Help me!" I screamed, before
a dirty hand that smelled like a sweaty crotch was placed
over my mouth.

"Hurry up, Barry. I want some of this bitch too." He took
ahold of my hands, pulled them over my head, and placed his
knees on the palms.

"Don't do that to that girl. That's a baby. You muthafuckas are sick!" the pretty woman screamed.

"Shut that dusty bitch up. She just mad 'cause don't nobody want her rotten box no more!" the man straddling me
ordered. He yanked down my pants and ripped my panties
from my frame with one hard tug, raising me a bit from the
wet concrete. I couldn't believe this was happening to me. I
was mortified, defenseless, and felt sick to my stomach.
These were addicts. I was sure they were carrying diseases.
Diseases I would probably not be able to get rid of. I

struggled to break free again and after confirming that I could not, I laid there and prayed for death. Cursing at the God who'd created me, only to go through the things that I had my entire life, I hated him for cursing and tormenting me. Tears ran out of my eyes. The man spread my legs further apart and ran his fingers up and down my privates, further annihilating my soul. I heard the sounds of his belt being unbuckled, and I closed my eyes and drifted off into a faraway mental land, where things like this never took place. There, me and the twins were blessed to have loving parents that never fought each other, but loved us and themselves, unconditionally. We were aligned under Christ, and our household was a safe haven. We never lived in the dangerous Red Hook Housing Projects, but had a nice four-bedroom house in Queens. I smiled, lost in the deepest recesses of my mind.

Chapter 6

Bentley

The rain crashed into my face. I could feel the blood from the injury of my kneecap drip down my leg, and into the socks and my shoes. But I ran faster and harder, constantly looking over my shoulder for Twelve and not seeing them. I ran into the backyard, and scaled the fence, landed on the other side then got to breaking down the alley at full speed.

After hitting it out of Asia's back door, and taking the stairwell down and out of the building, I was running as fast as I could. I wasn't about to go down for the shit with Asia, fuck that. My father knew damn well I hadn't popped his bitch, but I was almost certain he was telling the police I had, and I was sure they would believe him. I was eighteen, with three pistol cases on my juvenile record already, and one reckless endangerment to safety as an adult I'd caught, six months after my seventeenth birthday. My record said I was a menace with them cannons and in the state of New York that was all the police needed to bury you like a bone in the backyard. So, I wasn't going. They was gone have to kill me before I allowed them to lock me up for somethin' like that. I ran out of that alley, crossed a busy street after waiting for a bunch of cars to pass, and started to break down the next one.

The was rain was coming down so hard, it felt as if I were being pushed backwards. I was breathing harder than an angry bear. I got halfway down the alley when I saw a person running toward me. Behind them, a group of people were gathered. I brought my running to a jog, and went on alert.

The closer the person got, the clearer their words became. "Help. Help. They raping that baby. Please help her," the woman sobbed. Within seconds, I recognized her voice. My mother's.

"Mama?" I ran to her and pulled her into my arms. She felt lighter than the last time I'd held her there. "What's the matter? Who's raping who?"

She turned around and pointed. "Go, son! Go. She just a baby. Somebody's baby."

I looked past her shoulder to the group of people, wishing I had my pistol on me. I nodded. "Stay here, queen. I'll be right back." I kissed her soft cheek, and took off in a jog. Looking around for a weapon, I spotted a big two by four, about three yards from where I'd left my mother. I picked it up, and ran down the alley toward the group. "Hey! You bitch-ass muthafuckas! Leave her alone. Get the fuck away from her!" They appeared not to hear me, so when I got close enough, I swung the two by four as hard as I could and made contact with one of the men's backs that was standing there.

Crack!

He fell over the man that was on top of the girl, disrupting whatever he was trying to do. "Shit!" He stumbled to his feet and took off running, and so did the other man that had been holding her hands. The one that straddled her body jumped up with his pants pulled around his thighs. He looked panicked, and tried to pull his pants into place. But, before he could, I cracked him right along the side of the head with the board. It vibrated in my grasp.

He fell to his knees, then jumped up and took off running, with blood coming from his head. Stopped short and fell to his knees again, tried to get up and collapsed. I rushed to his side, and kicked him as hard as I could in his ribs. He rolled to his back, and curled into a ball. I stood there stomping him for the better part of a minute, until my mother pulled me off of him. Then he jumped up and took off running, falling every few feet.

The girl got up, and tried to run, slipped, and landed face first in a puddle. "Help me. Help me. Please somebody help me!" she screamed. She got to her feet and took off running.

I ran behind her. "Wait. Hey! Wait. You need to go to the hospital. Hey." She was running so fast, I had to switch into another gear. When I finally caught up to her, I grabbed her and fell to the ground with her, alongside of the Barbecue Pit dumpster. She got to fighting me like crazy right away.

"Get off of me! Get off of me! Help! Somebody!" she screamed.

Then it hit me, the face, the voice, my jacket. This was Jade. I'd found her in another sticky situation. I held her arms while she tried to fight me off of her. "Jade! Jade! Ma chill, it's me, Bentley. I ain't about to let shit else happen to you. That's my word."

She continued to fight for another ten seconds or so, then stopped and gave me a dumbfounded look. Her eyes were bucked. Her lips split. Slowly her face contorted into sorrow. "Bentley, they tried to rape me. They tried to hurt me so bad." She broke into a fit of sobs. Shaking, she hollered and scooted away from me and sat in another muddy puddle before coming to her feet.

I lowered my head and shook it. "I'm sorry this happened, Jade. Some muthafuckas just ain't right. But I swear, I'll never let nobody hurt you again. I swear, I'll protect you in any way I can." I stepped up to her, and tried to pull her into my embrace.

She took a step back and shook her head. "No. No. You're a man. You're just like them. You're just like them.

All men are." She backed against the dumpster. Her head clunked against the bar the garbage trucks used to elevate and dump it.

There was a loud whistle. The police drove past the alley, then slammed on their brakes. Backed up and flipped on their sirens, then turned into the far end of the alley, flooring it.

"Shit, ma! Let's go!" I grabbed her wrist and pulled her along. We took off running. Got halfway up the alley and ran through the gangway of a furniture store. Came out on to the busy street and broke across it, weaving through traffic. Once on the other side, we headed through another gangway. Jade was booking it. Running so fast she stumbled twice, but I was there to keep her up and at 'em. She kept running and I stayed behind her, as we heard the sirens get close. Lightning exploded in the sky. We wound up in another alley, running down it as fast as our bodies would allow.

My chest felt tight. There was a sharp pain in my left side. I felt ready to double over. We came out of that alley, and ran smack dead into a police car. It stopped right in front of us. The driver threw it in park, and got ready to jump out. He tried to open the door, but I kicked it back shut. "Keep running, Jade! Go ma, I'll catch up."

Jade ran across the street, and alongside of another gangway, then disappeared altogether. The policeman scooted across the console of his car, opened the other door, and took off running behind me. I went back in the direction we had come. Hopped two fences with him on my ass, circled back to the alley, and in the direction Jade had run. When I looked over my shoulder, Twelve was damn near fifty yards back. He clumsily slipped on the wet concrete and I thanked God in my head for small favors. Up ahead, Jade climbed over a fence and her jacket got caught on top of it.

Life of Sin

She landed halfway to the ground, but her jacket remained bound. I rushed over, breathing heavily, and freed her. She fell beside me, then jumped up, looking both ways. Her natural hair was matted to her beautiful face. She seemed to be near hysteria. I grabbed her shoulders. "Calm down, ma. Calm down, we gon come from under this. Come on." I reached for her hand, but she yanked hers away and backed up. "Jade, please. Just trust me. I swear I won't hurt you. Let's get out of here." The thunder roared. The rain came down twice as hard lightning flashed again. The wind blew so hard that I was having a hard time standing still. It threatened to knock me over.

She shook her head as the sirens got closer. A series of cars slammed on their brakes. I knew the law had to be in the area searching for us. Time was running out. I was beginning to panic. "Please, Jade, follow me." I reached for her hand again.

She shook her head. "No, just go. I'll follow you."

I nodded, and took off running. We were in somebody's backyard. From a distance, I could see police lights everywhere I looked. The alley was lit up. I assumed they were on the next block as well. We were trapped. There was no way to turn, so I ran and ducked down by the back porch of the yard we were in. "Come on, Jade, get under here. Twelve everywhere, we gotta wait 'em out. Hurry up."

She stood in place for a second, biting on her nail. Looked both ways, and backed up. The rain popped off of her head. "We should keep running. Getting under there is stupid."

I started to hear CB radios. That told me Twelve was closer than ever. I ran toward Jade and grabbed her wrist. "Man, come on, before they book you for a murder you didn't commit. Damn."

She relented, allowed me to guide her under the porch. I had her crawl all the way to the back, and then I joined her. Pulled her to me, and wrapped my arms around her. I held her even though I could feel her discomfort in our close quarters. I didn't understand why she was so cold to me this had been the second time I'd tried to save her from a fucked-up position. She made me feel lower than dirt. I sat there hugging her in discontentment, praying we overcame our current situation and knowing tomorrow would be another day.

Twelve traveled in and out of the backyard all night long. I was thankful they did not check under that porch. If they had, both Jade and I would have been caught and locked up for crimes that neither of us had committed.

***

"Yo, why you even getting involved wit this bitch, Dunn? Shorty linked to all kinds of trouble. Ya ass is already on the line for Asia's shooting. The Jakes been all over the building wit ya picture and shit. Now you wanna align wit a murder." Santana shook his head. "Just stupid." Two thick-ass Harlem bitches walked past in the hallway, smiled at me, and kept it moving. Their Daisy Dukes were all up in their asses. It looked good to me, I couldn't lie about that.

It was now the next day. Me and Jade had stayed under that porch all night, while Twelve went back and forth seemingly searching for us. It had gotten freezing cold at about three in the morning. That forced us to snuggle to each other, and she did so apprehensively. That had been the first time in a long time I'd spent the whole night holding a woman. I usually wasn't that type, only did things of the like when I was guilt tripped by Asia. But, there was something about Jade. I couldn't quite put my finger on it, but something deep within my soul somehow felt connected to her. I didn't like that feeling at all. "Yo, fuck them blue boys, kid. I ain't pop shorty. The cannon fell on the ground and it went off. That shit wasn't my fault. My old man just on some fuck shit wit that whole situation. I'll figure that out at a later date. But as far as she goes, yo, I ain't about to leave her out in the streets to get creased, nah mean? So, I'ma fuck wit her for a minute. That's just that. All I need is a banger, and a place we can lay our heads. Preferably somewhere remote. I'm thinking the Bronx or somethin', the law don't be sweating like that out there."

Santana shook his head again. "Nigga, you tripping. I got a cannon, but I don't know where y'all gon lay ya head at. All I know is trap spots. Band-os. I know you ain't trying to fuck wit none of them, I mean, are you?" He took a pull off the Newport he was smoking. Blew the smoke to the ceiling, and looked back at me with a slight smirk on his face.

"Yo, I'll take whatever right now. I just want shorty to be able to shower, and get her mind right. She been through a lot. She's traumatized."

Santana smiled. "I got you, Dunn, but I hope that don't stop us from bussing a few moves. I gotta get my cake right. We gotta handle some bidness. So, I'ma set y'all up, and give you a day or two to settle in, then me and you gon make some power moves to gross some capital. Tired of being broke, Blood, word up." One of the apartment doors opened up, this made Santana perk up. A Grecian female stepped out into the hallway, and signaled with her forefinger for him to come to her. "Yo, kid, I'ma fuck wit you in a minute. Let me hit this gyro thing off, then I'ma holla back in about an hour."

"You know I don't like when you say racist shit like that, Santana. I'm not a fucking food, I'm Greek. There is a difference."

He grabbed her by the waist, then hugged up on her. "Bitch, shut up. You know I'm about to turn you into a meal anyway." They proceeded to tongue each other down.

**

When I got back inside Santana's crib, Jade was sitting on the couch, staring off into space. She stood up as I stepped into the room. "Bentley, I appreciate you for helping me last night, but I gotta get out of here so I can figure some things out for myself. The cops are looking for me. I can't be in New York, it's not safe. I need to make some money, so I can get a lawyer to clear my name. Once I do, I gotta find my sisters, and get them back. The foster care system in New York is horrible, from what I've googled."

"Yo, I know what mission lies ahead for you and I wanna help, but before we do anything else, you gotta get cleaned up, get you some sleep and restore yourself. Right now you're running on fumes. You're going to self-destruct. Now, my mans about to find us a nice duck-off out in the Bronx. I say we lay low for a while, then get on this new journey. Besides, I got some shit on my plate as well. Both our backs are against the wall. We gotta figure things out. Just please, come with me. I don't want you out in those streets alone. It's not safe."

She bit on her forefinger looked uneasy. "Why do you care so much, Bentley? Huh? I don't know what you think you're about to get from me, but in case you haven't noticed, I don't have anything. I'm dirt poor without a lot to piss in, so before you decide to put me up for a spell, you need to factor all of that in."

I stepped toward her. "Look, Jade, you need to quit it wit that punk-ass attitude. I don't want shit from you. I'm trying to protect you from that cold world out there. You can't beat it alone. Nobody can. But, if you keep acting the way you're acting then you're going to be forced to. And I care, because I know you got dealt a shitty hand. I know you didn't kill your father. Your mother admitted to doing it right in my face. It's not fair that she's trying to blame it on you. Trying to throw you in jail for the rest of your natural life. That's fucked up. Only a bitch would do some shit like that."

"Don't you call my mother out of her name. You don't know her or what all she's been through. You sound like my fucking father." She said this, pointing her pinky at me. Defensive, her nostrils flared. She honestly looked so fine, angry.

I held my hands up. "I'm sorry. I didn't mean it."

"Yeah, he never meant it either. That's what all men say." She turned her back to me and walked to the window, pulled the curtain back and looked out of it. "I don't need another man looking over me. It's only a matter of time before you're trying to beat my ass, or force yourself upon me. Y'all all alike. Fucking cavemen," she scoffed, and exhaled loudly.

I felt offended. "Jade, I ain't that nigga. So don't be putting that fuck shit yo pops or however many other niggas did to you, on me. I sweat clowns like those. Stomp 'em into the ground and piss on they bitch-ass. I'm a real nigga, cut from a whole different cloth. Get that shit right. Word up."

She turned around to face me and walked over until she was standing about two feet away from me. "What's your end game wit me, Bentley? Huh? I'm broken. Ain't got no family. Mother turned on me. Sisters snatched by the city.

Warrants out for my arrest. Broke as a homeless person in debt. So what do you want wit me? I am a liability to you. Not an asset, and ain't that what all you dope boys are about, a fucking asset?" She stepped closer, challenging me.

I stared at her for a long time. Even with the mud caked in her hair and all over her face, the stale breath, and the scent of urine coming from her clothes, she was still bad to me. I swear I could see the diamond under all that rough. And trust me, she looked rougher than sandpaper. I knew she was hurting. Lashing out at the first available man she could clap at and him having to be me sucked, because I kind of liked her, but her attitude was getting the best of me.

"Man, Jade, I know you hurting right now and I'm trying to take that into consideration, but on the real, you making shit way harder than it gotta be. I'm trying to help yo stubborn ass. Damn!"

"You ever stop to think that I don't trust yo ass, or no-body like you. Nigga, you's a project thug. Y'all lie, cheat, steal, and hurt people. I ain't buying this facade, or whatever the fuck you putting on for me. I know you're up to no good. The only thing I wanna know is where do I fit in, in the grand scheme of things."

I balled up my face, and got disgusted. She'd basically just called me scum to my face. Told me I wasn't shit. That bruised my ego more than a pretty bitch spitting in my face and calling me ugly. "Yo, you know what, I had it up to here, shorty. Fuck you. You wanna take ya ass out there and fight in them streets alone, then go. Good riddance." I walked to the front door and opened it, ready to throw her ass out. I was over her already. Needed to get her out of my sight, so I could focus on my own shit I had going on.

"Cool. I don't need you. Have a nice life." She stormed past me on her way into the hallway, when Santana came rushing toward us. He grabbed her and pulled her back inside. She smacked at his hands. "Get off of me."

Santana tossed her toward the couch. "Yo, the law just pulled on the block, like eight cars deep. They parked right up the way, so y'all gotta get out of here. Come on." He ran to the back of the house after dipping in and out of both bedrooms, handed me a duffle bag and some car keys. "Take that whip that's parked in the alley. I'll text you in a few minutes, we gon meet back up in Harlem, kid, now go."

I headed down the fire escape, but stopped, and looked for Jade. She stood frozen at the top of the stairs. "Yo, come on, Jade. I'm sorry for snapping at you. Shit just crazy right now, we both need some rest. But, time is of the essence." I held my hand out to her. You rolling?"

Chapter 7

Jade

I dunked the wash rag into the bucket filled with bleach and Pine Sol for the hundredth time, pulled it back out and wrung it out over the bucket, before wiping down the rest of the living room wall with it. Me and Bentley had cleaned the whole house two times from top to bottom, and after the disaster we'd walked into, it was starting to look like a place I could lay my head for a few weeks. I stood up and looked around, satisfied with the results.

Bentley opened the front door and came inside, carrying a bag of KFC, and a two-liter soda. "Yo, I got the old head from up the block coming through later. He gon see if he can get this electricity turned on by bussing a few moves. We might have to spend one more night in the dark though. I got a bunch of candles in the car. I'll be right back." He sat the bag of food on the table and stepped out of the apartment, closing the door behind him.

After leaving Santana's place, we'd driven straight to this place in Harlem. When we got here, the apartment was packed with a bunch of heroin addicts. Santana followed us over and when he got here, he kicked them all out and moved them upstairs to his uncle's trap, where I guess they'd been ever since. There had been nonstop knocking on the door the entire night. Bentley answered it and sent them to the new location each time with a bit of an attitude. I was thankful he had.

I exhaled loudly, and looked around the small place where I'd be residing for a short period, or at least until I could get my plans in order. It was a one-bedroom apartment, with a tiny living room, and kitchen. The walls were peeling, and there appeared to be a bit of a roach problem. I hadn't seen any rats yet, but I was sure there were some lurking in the weeds, waiting for an opportune time to come out and scavenge for a morsel of food. The electricity was off, and we were temporarily keeping things cold by the use of a cooler we'd packed with ice from the bodega on the corner. The gas worked, but there was no stove. Thankfully, it was late August, and the weather hadn't reached the freezing cold stage as of yet. Bentley had purchased a bunch of comforters, sheets, and blankets. He'd moved in a queen sized bed early this morning, and had it set up in the bedroom. I didn't know what his intentions were for buying it, but if it was for both of us to share, that wasn't happening. I would much rather sleep right on the worn couch in the living room. I'd scrubbed it as best I could and drenched it in Febreeze, before allowing it to dry and covering it with a sheet. While I was thankful for everything he was doing for us, especially on my behalf, I was nowhere near ready to go there with him. Not only did my body hurt, but my heart ached. My emotions were all out of whack. My weight had dropped considerably. I was constantly paranoid. I worried about my sisters. I worried about my mother. I worried what would happen to me once I was apprehended. And I was scared of what the future held. Every noise, every person, everything spooked me. I saw the bad in it and prepared for the pain, or the attacks that would come from it. It felt like there was a dark cloud looming over me, as if the Reaper of death stood behind my back, waiting impatiently for my demise. I was miserable and didn't know what to do, other than roll with the punches. I had to find a way capitalize off of Bentley before he turned into my father. I knew there was only a matter of time before he did.

Bentley came back into the house and closed the door. He was carrying two bags, both from Walmart. "Yo, you got it smelling real good in here, Jade. That hallway lit though." He laughed, and stepped into the kitchen, sat the bags on the table and began to rifle through them. "Yo, I ain't know what kind of cereal you liked, so I just got a couple boxes of Cap'n Crunch, and these Cookie Crisp joints my mom likes. I don't know if all females do or not, but they here whenever you want 'em." He took the gallon of milk, knelt down and rifled through the ice in the cooler, before setting the milk all the way at the bottom of it, and covering it back. Then he did the exact same thing with a carton of orange juice as well. The light from the window in the living room shimmered off the top of his deep waves. It looked as if he'd just gotten his hair cut. His goatee was nicely lined. I could tell that he was a well out together person, at least on the outside. Internally, he was still a mystery to me. I had yet to find out what his hidden agenda was. He started to take more contents out of the bags. I saw sugar, seasonings, paper plates, plastic utensils, soap and two different kinds of deodorant, there was also all kinds of food products that didn't need refrigeration. "Damn, it smell good in here though."

I took a deep breath and slowly exhaled, trying to calm my nerves. I still felt quite uneasy around him, but I saw that he was at least trying to be nice. It wouldn't kill me to do the same. When an opportunity presented itself, then I would make my move. "Yeah, I been cleaning all day. I mean, I know we kind of got to it before you left, but I just felt that it needed a lil more work, so that's what I've been doing since you left here this morning. I hit the bathroom again, the living room, and the bedroom. I feel better."

He turned and smiled. "That's most important." Came out of the kitchen and handed me a toothbrush, Crest toothpaste, and a stick of Suave deodorant. "I know these ain't the best living arrangements, but you know what, it's better than being in jail. We gone figure things out, Jade, trust me. I gotta get my hand on some paper. Once I get our money right we'll be able to move out of New York and to bigger and better thang. It's just a process." He went back to messing around with the groceries. Unpacking them and putting things into cabinets.

I held the items that he'd given me to my chest. I felt dirty because I had not paid for them. I knew that nothing came free in the world. I wondered what he expected in return for them. "Uh, Bentley, whose place is this? And how long are they going to allow for us to stay here?"

He came out of the kitchen, and set a bunch of candles on the table. The thick kind, that looked like a tree trunk. "Aw, it's good. This is one of Santana's uncle's places. He owns the building. He's a bit of a slum lord, but he gave us the go-ahead to stay here for a lil while. I'ma hit his hand at the end of the week. Santana already got him right already, so no worries, ma. All you gotta do is lean back, and get your mind right. We got a helluva journey ahead, but in order to make it we have to be well rested."

"And for these items, and that food in there? What do I owe you for them?" I wanted to know what he expected before I ate or brushed my teeth with the things he'd bought. I didn't want to find myself in the hole or with a bill I wasn't willing to pay.

He frowned, stared at me for a second and laughed. "Yo, you wilin', queen. You gotta let your guard down just a lil bit. I ain't looking to jam you up. I ain't the enemy. Everything that I went out and bought is for us. No strings, no bill attached. We in this shit together. Just a couple project kids, trying to figure life out, right?" He peered into my eyes with his caramel brown ones. I could smell a hint of his cologne. Being so close I was able to make out where the barber had been a tad too rough with his edging. There were a few scratches along his forehead that were made by the barber's hair clippers. I wondered if they hurt. Bentley seemed like the type that would ignore pain. Like the type that would fight through as long as he was able to meet his goal on the other side of it. His demeanor was that of pure determination. My situation was a perfect example. For as long as he and I had been in rotation, I had not made things easy, yet he ignored the ill treatment of him and stayed the course. What course? I was unsure. I had yet to figure this man out.

I nodded. "I guess that's a cool way of looking at it, but I'm letting you know right now that as soon as the heat dies down, I am going to go out and get a job so I can reimburse you for everything you've bought on my behalf. I don't need nobody to do for me like I'm handicapped or something, so just know this is a temporary loan. You dig me?"

He nodded. "On some real shit, a simple thank you would be enough for me. This is peanuts to an elephant. I just wanted to get us the basics. Can't have us walking around starving, and funky, nah mean? At the end of the day we're still human, we're in fucked-up positions, but we're still human. You don't owe me nothing, Jade." He walked back into the kitchen and started messing with the cupboards again. "Yo, I'ma go out and buss a few moves wit Santana later. Once I get a bag, I'ma snatch you up so I can take you shopping. Buy you a couple 'fits. I know you tired of wearing that same old outfit. I know you need some under things too, I don't know ya sizes, so look forward to that trip. Aiight? If there is anything else I can get for you, let me know."

I stood there perplexed. I didn't know what to say or to think. I wish I could read what was going on inside his head. I wanted to know if he saw me as a charity case. Did he think I was incapable of providing for myself? That I was some kind of recluse or something? Why did he feel the need to do everything for me? He had to be up to something. All the years of my life, I never saw my father do anything nice for my mother. He never took the initiative to cater to her needs. It was all about him. All about his wants, needs and desires. I knew that every male was like that. They were all selfish, abusive, and sly predators. They all had hidden agendas, Bentley was no different. I would figure out what he was up to sooner than later, then I would flip the script on him and leave on top. But once again, in the moment, I was willing to play my role. "That sounds good, Bentley. I'd really appreciate that."

"Don't even mention it. Now, let's tear up this chicken before it gets too cold." He squirted a nice portion of hand sanitizer into his palm and rubbed it all around, then gave it to me and I did the same thing.

We sat down at the table. He placed a big bucket of crispy chicken in the center, and alongside of it were all the fixings. It smelled so good, my stomach started growling like a like a pitbull, ready to strike. Everything looked so good. The scent was amazing. I took a big piece of paper towel and opened it on my lap, grabbed a paper plate, and waited for him to grab his food first. In our household, my father was always the first to be served. After him, then came the twins and myself. My mother took her portion last. I felt that was the way of the world, so it blew my mind when he looked over at me and told me to go first. I was so taken aback, I sat frozen in place. "What?"

Life of Sin

He smiled. "Ladies first. My mother taught me to always feed the queen in the room before myself." He paused and looked around. "Seeing as though you are the only queen in the room, you should go first. But hurry up, 'cause I'm hungry as hell." I could tell he was serious about that, as he laid his paper towel across his napkin.

I felt real awkward reaching into the bucket before him, first, because I didn't pay for the food and secondly, because he was the man. I was raised to know that men were to be served before the women and children, so this was kind of odd, but I was so hungry I shrugged that off and grabbed me two pieces, one breast and a drumstick, which were my favorite. Spooned some macaroni and cheese on to my paper plate, and took a soft, mouth-watering biscuit. I waited for him to grab his two breasts and drumstick, macaroni, coleslaw and a biscuit, before I slid my hands across the table.

He gave me a look that told me he was confused. "Yo, you tryna steal my food, ma?" He twisted the cap from the two-liter bottle of soda pop, poured some into a paper cup, and slid it across the table to me.

I shook my head. "Do you mind if we give thanks? I mean, I know it may not seem like we have much to be thankful for, but we have to appreciate God's small blessings. We are alive and well." I avoided eye contact with him, already starting to feel rejected. I felt stupid, but I feared Jehovah.

He sucked his teeth. "Yo, God been forgot about me, shorty. He don't mess with me and I don't mess with him, or her, or whatever is up, or down there. I just live in the moment. That religion shit is a ploy for mafuckas to get rich off the backs of the poor and ill-advised, those of us looking for a savior. That ain't me. I'ma make shit happen for myself. No disrespect."

"None taken, now give me your hands, because I wanna bless our food and say thank you. Your utter lack of faith has nothing to do with my beliefs and appreciation of him. So hand them over. I'm not taking no for an answer."

He frowned, and sighed. "Aiight, forget it. Have it your way." He handed them to me and closed his eyes, shaking his head.

I smiled. "Father, in the mighty name of Jesus, we thank you for this meal that you have set before us. We ask that you bless this meal. Please protect us from any impurities. Thank you for always making a way out of no way. Amen." I released his warm, big hands and opened my eyes. He was staring right at me with his head turned sideways. That made me blush.

"Soooo, can we eat now, or?" he asked, mocking me.

I giggled and caught myself. "Yeah, you can eat. Be thankful that God ain't gon let you choke now. If you only had the slightest idea of how much you're saved on a daily basis, you'd retract that last statement you made. But, no judging over here. I'ma pray for you." I picked up my drumstick and bit into it. The food was lukewarm at this point, but it was better than nothing. The taste was still KFC, and it was mmmm-mmmm-good.

Bentley dove into his food without wasting any time. "Yo, I ain't mean to offend your religion or nothin', I just don't believe in all that jazz. Too much bad shit be happening on a daily for there to be a God up there. If there is some kind of higher power sitting back watching while all of this cruel shit goes on down here, and could stop it but don't, then we're all in trouble. Yo, I ain't no God or nothin', but I'd never let nothin' happen to a lil kid, or a defenseless female. Word is bond, that's just sick."

I swallowed my food. "You can't blame everything that happens bad on God. There is an evil force out there called the devil, don't forget about that. There's also a thing called free will. God granted free will to all of his children at the beginning of time. So, even though he can stop people from doing evil, he doesn't because it's their own free will to do so. Besides, this world ain't his kingdom, his kingdom is above. This world will pass away, and that will be that. All if the choices that men made on it will affect them after this planet dies and his kingdom is the final dwelling place. Well, his and hell. It's complicated, but if you'd like, we can get a Bible and study a bit." I took a sip of my soda, looking over the rim at him.

He had a mouthful of chicken. "No, thank you. I'ma take your word for it and leave it at that. Whether he up there or not, it ain't gon save us from our current situation. We gotta figure this out on our own. That's just that." He commenced to chowing down like he was really hungry, and because he ate like a savage, I stopped trying to be all prim and proper, and ate like I was starving too. When it was all said and done, we burped the same time. That made me blush.

***

That night, his guy had been unable to get the electricity turned on and on top of that, the neighborhood was experiencing its own blackout from the thunderstorm. We set up the living room with a bunch of candles, threw the pillows from the couch on the floor, and sat across from one another, after finishing off the KFC from earlier. The whole time I thought the apartment had at least had the gas on, but I found out it did not this night. Since it was raining so hard outside, this made the inside cold. I shook like a leaf. Wrapped a sheet around my shoulders, and waited for him to be seated. I knew he was set to leave with Santana soon, but I didn't know when. I was just thankful I didn't have to be alone right then.

He sat on the floor and smiled over at me as he held a thick candle in his hand. "Yo, at least we ain't the only ones sitting in the dark right now. All of the electricity from 145th to 149th and Broadway is out." For some reason, that made me feel a lil better." His shadow danced on the wall behind him. Even in the candlelight, he looked handsome. I tried not to notice.

"Okay, so what are we going to do? It's nine something, raining like crazy, and we're stuck indoors with no technology. Seems rough, Bentley."

He pulled out his phone. "You wanna watch a movie on Netflix until Santana hits me up? I'll even let you pick it. I don't mind the chick flicks," he snickered.

I rolled my eyes and grabbed his phone. Saw it was on forty percent battery life and decided against it. "Watching a movie would deplete your battery. If your phone is dead, how will Santana get in contact with you?"

He nodded. "Damn, you right." He looked off in thought, then looked me over. "I'm saying, I know you ain't tryna—"

"No," I cut him off, already knowing where that request was headed. Sex was the last thing on my mind. A part of me wanted to get to know him. I wanted to begin to understand the man underneath it all. "How about we talk for a minute, I got some questions for you, that cool?"

He licked his thick lips. "Aiight, but only if I can ask you a few too. Deal?"

"Deal."

90

Life of Sin

Chapter 8

Jade

"What is your favorite food?" I didn't really care, but I wanted to see how he looked when he was telling the truth, that way I could begin to understand and peep his tells.

"Really, ma, you wanna know that? We ain't even got no stove for you to cook it, if you did know." He started laughing. His deep dimples were prominent on his jaws.

"That's what I wanna know, so spill the info." I smiled at him, couldn't help it. It felt good to do so as well.

"Yo, if I had to pick one thing it would definitely be lasagna. I'm talking triple cheese with that good ground beef, not the ground chuck, nah mean. Second to lasagna is pizza, but that goes without saying. What about you?"

I shook my head. "That's my favorite too. I love lasagna. It makes me feel as if I'm getting away with something because it has multiple layers, it's so good and extremely filling. But, my second favorite food is shrimp."

"I don't like shrimp, seafood ain't really anything. Fish is cool, but I don't like that slimy shit. I can't even swim," he admitted, pulling a blunt from his shirt pocket, licking it, then setting fire to it. The smoke was strong, attacked my nose right away. I backed away from him. He must've noticed, because he held the smoke in his lungs and backed up. "Damn, my bad. You don't smoke?"

I shook my head. "Nall, I never have before. My mother would've beat my ass. All my friends talked about it at school, but I never indulged. But it's cool, do your thing, next question."

He looked at the blunt, took six quick pulls and stubbed it out in the ashtray that was sitting next to him. "Shoot."

"Are you an only child?"

"Far as I know. Do you and the twins all have the same father?" he asked, sipping from the orange juice he'd taken out of the cooler and poured into a paper cup.

"Yeah, my mother is a real loyal person. She loved my father with all her heart and I'm sure never cheated on him. If she had, I would have been the first person she confessed it to." I reached for the bag of cups and the sheet fell off my shoulders. The blouse was so worn by this point, the collar was stretched horribly. I felt a cool chill go down the back of my shirt. I grabbed the cups and held a cup up for Bentley to pour me some. He filled it halfway, then stopped. I shot him a confused look, raised my left eyebrow.

"Can I ask you a question?" he asked, pouring a tad bit more of the juice and looking down at it. He replaced it inside the cooler, came back over and sat down.

I took a sip and swished it around in my mouth, swallowed and closed my eyes. "Go ahead."

He took a deep breath. "When you just bent over just now, I saw down your shirt, and..."

I tensed up. Here we go. Now he was about to tell me how good my breasts looked, and how they made him feel some type of way. And explain to me why I should sleep with him. I knew it was coming. It had all been just a matter of time. I got pissed off and ready to snap. I glared at him with obvious anger.

"If you don't want to talk about it, it's cool, I'll stay in my lane," he ended.

Fuck, I had not even heard what game he tried to run and that was even more irritating.

"Talk about what? I didn't hear you," I said, flaring my nostrils.

He leaned forward and whispered, "The scars on your back. I said I saw them when you leaned over just now, and earlier when you were bent over, scrubbing the lower portion of the wall. Do you care to talk about them?"

A chill went down my spine. I sat back and fixed the collar to my blouse and pulled the sheet more snug around me. I felt embarrassed. Caught. Like an outcast. And most importantly, vulnerable. "I'd rather we didn't."

He stuttered his words. "I-I-I didn't mean to intrude. I wanted to ask you about them earlier, but I ain't have the nerve, plus you and I weren't really on speaking terms. You were kind of giving me the cold shoulder." He grabbed a pillow and sat down on it, situating himself for comfort. His shadow danced on the wall behind him, illuminated by the flame of the candles. We made eye contact, and then his eyes averted from my own. There was a silence in the room. I could tell he didn't know where to go after my answer. "Did I just ruin the mood?"

"Nall, there was no mood to ruin. I just wish you would-n't be so nosey. What's on my body is my business. Damn." I scrunched my nose, and turned away from him.

He sat there for a little while longer, then stood up. Start-ed to send a text on his phone, before shutting it off. "Shorty, on my mother, I'm so sick of yo fuckin' attitude. All you do is bitch, bitch, bitch. That shit getting real old. Straight up. You making it real hard for me to relate to you in any way. I ain't no humble nigga like this to every bitch. Trust me." He mugged me, and snatched his pillow from the floor.

I jumped up. "You need to watch yo mouth. I ain't no bitch. I don't care what them other hoez out there let you call them, but I ain't them. I'ma queen, check yaself." I was heated, and ready for him to whoop my ass like my father always did my mother. I knew I deserved it. Women weren't supposed to talk to men the way I just had, but I refused to allow for him to call me a bitch, or to treat me disrespectfully. I would not be as weak of a woman as my mother had been. I would set a precedent.

He balled his hands into fists. I prepared for the inevitable blow that was sure to come, readied myself for his physical rage. He would probably beat me. Then kick me out into the freezing rain. I would be sick and homeless, but at least I would have my pride.

He exhaled loudly, and ran both hands over his face. His right one held his iPhone. "Uh! Fuck!" He took his hands away and looked at the ceiling. "I was wrong for that. You ain't no bitch, ma. I apologize for my insinuations. I ain't mean it like that to begin wit, but nevertheless, you had a right to check me on it. You are a queen, and you've been through a lot. I was just concerned, that's all. It won't happen again. I'll stay on my side of the highway." His phone vibrated. He read the message. "Yo, that's Santana right there. I'ma go fuck with Blood, then catch you later. I'ma leave my phone wit you too, just in case you need to call me for anything. After I hit this lick, I'ma cop you one. I should be back in a few hours. I know you don't care, but I just had to let you know what's good. Do you need anything while I'm out?" Lightning flashed across the curtains, before the familiar thunder played its role. The noise sent my hairs standing on end. I'd always hated thunderstorms.

"Nall, I don't need nothin'. I guess I'll see you when you get back."

He sat his phone on the table, and the worst possible thing happened. My cycle decided to drop right there and it was unfortunate, because I was standing right in front of six candles in a pair of beige pants. The blood was undeniable. Now I wished I had stood up with the sheet wrapped around me. Bentley eyed my crotch, but didn't say a word. "Well, I'll see you later then."

***

Bentley

"Yo, kid, this move gon be nice and easy. I got this British kat named Barron that stay in Queens, he own this Mercedes Benz dealership and whatnot. He get all of them new joints as soon as they come out. Have 'em sent from overseas straight to his dealership. Anyway, he just got a shipment on 2020 hard-drop Benzes in three days ago, it's ten of them. He want us to go on his lot and snatch them bitches, so he can collect the insurance. He got this scam going where every time his shit get hit, Mercedes Benz reimburse him for the purchase of the vehicles taken, then his insurance pay him that same amount as well. So, it's like he wind up getting the car for free. He get paid from both, get a new whip, and get to sell it at his sticker price."

"And the rich get richer," I chimed in, with Jade still on my mental. "So, what's the word? We about to take ten of them in one night?" I didn't mind, we'd done jobs with more work, and had less time to do it. All I cared about was the money involved. I needed to get me and Jade right. My mother's rent was coming up in a few days too. I had to make sure I paid it, and the rest of her bills. If I didn't, then who would? I took the Dutch out the inside pocket of my fatigue jacket, licked it up and down, before lighting the end. I had so many things swarming through my brain, I could barely think clearly. I was hoping the loud would calm me down just a bit. It usually did.

Santana opened the ashtray slot, and pulled out a Dutch that was half gone. Placed it to his lips, and grabbed my lighter from me. "Yeah, we gone snatch all ten of them bitches and roll them to this garage out in Brooklyn. It's a couple blocks down from Coney Island. Kid 'nem already airing on these joints." Big tufts of dark smoke wafted from his cigar. It smelled strong and rich. He took three quick pulls and inhaled them all at once.

"What they gon do wit 'em at the garage? It like a chop shop or somethin'? And, if so, I know a way better one down the street from Marcy in Bed-Stuy. We can make ten thousand a piece for each whip, that's two hunnit bands right there. Especially if this British mafuckas gon get rid of them anyway." I took a pause to take a few tokes of my buddah. It already had me feeling some type of way. I felt calmer, yet at the same time, I couldn't get Jade off my mind. I knew it was her time of the month. It was storming like crazy and all the stores were closed. The only open place that potentially sold her feminine products would have been the twenty-four-hour CVS on 138th. It would've been hell trying to make it there in the storm. I felt real bogus for leaving her like that. I wondered how she was going to take care of her needs, without me making it happen for her? I blew out the smoke and pulled from the cigar again.

Santana shrugged his shoulders. "Bruh, I don't know why he got us dropping them shops off there, but those are my orders, so that's what we gon do. After we handle this bidness, then we gon meet up with these bitches. Keri been wiling over you, son, word up. Every time she come through Harlem, she ask about you. Say you snubbing her and all of that. Word." He laughed, and tried to give me his blunt. "Huh kid, this that Miami Red. This shit come straight from

Haiti. It's fye, gon have yo ass all the way on point. Trust me. Just try it."

I nudged his hand away. "Nah, son, I'm good wit this loud I got. I'll fuck wit you later on that shit. I ain't trying to be bussing no moves too lifted, nah' mean. That lead to mistakes." That was the spiel I gave him, but the truth was that Santana had a habit of making his blunts too wet on the ends. I ain't like exchanging spit wit another nigga, so if I had my own bud, I only smoked after me, unless I was blowing wit a cutie. Then, the whole spit exchange didn't bother me that much. I just didn't fuck wit niggas on that level, not even Santana and he was like my brother.

"Yeah aiight, suit yaself. I got a pound of this back at the telly anyway. 'Bout time we get there, shorty 'nem should be nice and faded. Let's handle this bidness first though, god, play later."

I nodded my head to the Cam'ron coming out of his speakers. Killa Cam was from Harlem, and I fucked wit his music tough. It was like kid spoke to my soul. "No doubt, bruh, let's make it happen."

Right after those words came out of my mouth, Santana drove down the strip to the Mercedes Benz dealership. The thunderstorm had picked up steam. It was raining so hard, it sounded like hail hitting the top of the roof. The car rocked from side to side, and lightning sparked in the sky every few seconds. The streets were flooded with water. As he drove, it splashed up along the side of our windows. I started to feel nervous as I looked across the street to the well-lit parking lot of the dealership. "Yo, you sure doing this tonight is smart?"

He turned off his system and circled around the boulevard. "Bruh, it gotta be tonight. I'm tryna get paid first thing in the morning. Let's do this shit."

Five minutes later, after circling around twice, he pulled into an alley in back of the dealership, and put his whip in park. Grabbed a small duffle bag full of utensils off the back seat, and unzipped it. "What all you need from this party kit? I got everything." He looked up to me and smiled.

I took my ski mask, and slid it over my face. "All I need is wire cutters, and a flat-head screwdriver. You can have everything else. Know yo skills ain't up to par," I joked, and grabbed the tools I needed. "You know where they at?"

He pulled out his phone, and looked over some kind of map. Tapped the screen three times to zoom into it, then looked it over closely. The thunder roared louder. The sound of the rain hitting the pavement resonated in my ears. "Aiight, all ten are parked on the east side of the lot."

"The east side? Shit, where are we?" I was getting mildly frustrated, because he was looking like he didn't know what the hell he was looking up. I never liked being the one that followed. I liked to be in charge, because I really didn't trust nobody but me. Santana's methods were always all over the place to me, whereas I was more calculating and precise. I didn't make many mistakes, because I had a knack for seeing things ahead of time and figuring them out before I got there.

"B, it's good, we on the north side of the lot. All of the trucks gon be through this lil pathway when we get out. We just head east, and the first ten Benzes we gon see is them. The sticker a' give 'em away anyway. Let's mob out." He slid his mask on and pulled his hood over his head. A hood had been the one thing I'd failed to come with, but I couldn't trip now, I had to roll wit the elements.

I opened the door and stepped out into the violent rain. The wind blew with so much force, I had to shield my eye holes because the water was crashing into the pupils of my eyes, almost attacking them. I ran behind Santana. My clothes were sticking to me, along with the cotton mask. We stomped through big puddles. My Timbs filled with water immediately. By the time we made it through and around the big lot, I was so irritated that I wanted to call the whole mission off. Santana ran around to a platinum 2020 Benz, and I chose a black on black one that looked fresh from the outside. I looked both ways before trying the door handle. The passenger's side was locked. I squatted back down, pulled out the screwdriver, and placed it into the lip of the back window, getting ready to jam it all the way in there so I could flick my wrist and shatter the glass, when I saw Santana scurry around to the driver's side of his car, and open the door with no problem. He jumped inside his whip and got right to work. I could see his head go under the dash because of the light shining from the poles of the dealership.

I decided to take his approach. I ran around to the driver's side of the black on black Benz and tried the handle of the door. It popped right open. I smiled under my mask and hopped inside. Ducked my head under the dash and took the screwdriver, placed it into the neck of the steering column, and broke a small rectangular piece, where I knew the fuse box, and all the connections to the wires were. Once they were exposed, I took the wire cutters and grabbed the purple and orange wires, clipped them, and stripped the coating off them with my teeth to expose the cooper-colored wires. Once they were exposed, I tapped them into each other a few times. The engine turned over, and the steering wheel popped loose. I made sure I could make full revolutions, before I tied the wires together and backed out of the parking space, just a few seconds after Santana did. That irritated me because I should have been able to handle my bidness faster than him, but I swore to myself that the next four cars would be done swifter.

He pulled out of the lot with me right behind him. The Benz felt like a million dollars. It handled well and felt light. The dashboard was lit up like a space ship. I threw the seat belt around me and stayed as close to him as I possibly could, with a major rush of adrenalin shooting through me. In two minutes, we were on the highway headed for the Bronx, with the rain beading against the windshield. *One down, four more trips to make*, I thought.

***

Jade

I curled up on the couch and gritted my teeth as another cramp shot through me. My stomach felt bloated. My head hurt and once again, I felt helpless. I had to get my ass up and make it to the store. I didn't like the feel of the tissue paper stuffed between my legs. It didn't last long enough to give me any sense of relief. Within minutes it was soggy and needed to be changed. I felt so uncomfortable. I hated life and wondered why I had been dealt such an impossible hand. I forced myself to sit up, then slowly came to my feet, squeezing my thighs together. Another cramp nearly hobbled me. Not only were my cramps horrible during my time of the month, but my flow remained heavy for the first three days.

There was only a fourth of a roll of tissue, and I knew it wouldn't last me more than another half-hour. The only set of pants I had was ruined. I'd washed them out, and they were hanging by the back window. I wanted to do the same thing with my underwear, but that would have been too embarrassing. I didn't want Bentley to see my panties hanging up to dry. The pants would be embarrassing enough. I'd already come on my cycle in front of him, though I wasn't sure if he actually saw or not. So, there I was with a sheet wrapped around me, with no change of clothes, and no sanitary napkins to stop my flow from spilling everywhere. I felt so defeated, so miserable.

I dropped the sheet, headed to the bathroom and ran the shower, got it as cool as I could, then stepped out of there to check the condition of my pants. I picked them up, only to find them dripping wet. The rain from outside had managed to attack them, leaving them soaking wet. There was a huge puddle of water on the floor right under the window. I cursed under my breath and threw the pants around my shoulder, just as the blood oozed down my thigh, further pissing me off. I looked toward the heavens and had to bite my tongue. "Lord, why me? Why me, Father? Ain't I suffering enough?"

I jetted into the bathroom and sat on the toilet, pulled the soppy tissue out of me, before using the bathroom and wiping myself clean. Flushed the toilet and stepped into the shower with my mind made up. I didn't care if the pants were wet. I didn't care if it was storming outside. I was going out to get me some tampons. There was a ten-dollar-bill on the table and I was going to use it. If Bentley got pissed at me, I didn't care. He didn't have the slightest idea of how bad we women had it. I lowered my head as the water beat on the back of my neck, then the tears started to flow heavily. Life was so shitty. I didn't feel like going out into that storm. I hated lightning. Thunder terrified me. Plus, I didn't know this area of Harlem. I knew it was horrible though, known for gang violence. I didn't want to be caught in the middle of more danger. Every time I tried to set out on my own, something bad always took place. I hated Bentley for leaving me alone. Hated him for leaving me to fend for myself in a house without power. What type of man was he? He was nothing more than a version of my heartless father. I hated him so much. More blood drained out of me. I spread my legs and allowed for the water to hit my kitty in a straight shot, washing me clean. The water was so cold that I felt tortured. I hated this life. I truly did.

After I got as clean as I possibly could, I hopped out of the shower, determined. I stuffed my feminine place with as much tissue as I could stand. Then, threw on the wet pants, the same blouse and my shoes, and bomber jacket. Took the ten dollars off the table, and prepared myself for the thunderstorm, when Bentley opened the door to the house and rushed in. I jumped back out of shock.

He carried a plastic Walgreen's bag in his hand. "Yo, I'm in the middle of this move, Jade, but I couldn't finish it without getting these to you. Yo, I ain't know the sizes or nothing, so I just got tampons in each size, and for each flow. I also got you these lil cheap jogging pants for now. I'ma take you shopping in the morning. I'm sorry I took so long." He sat the bag on the floor. All the power and stuff will be on tomorrow. I gotta get back to work, I'll holler at you later." Then, he opened the door and left.

I picked up the bag and looked inside of it. It was filled with tampons and toilet tissue. I smiled and shook my head. I didn't know what to say about Bentley. He had me so confused, I didn't know what to do, think, or feel. It terrified me.

Chapter 9

Bentley

Santana stopped outside the hotel room door and smiled with two bottles of Ace of Spades in his hands. "Yo, everything went smooth, kid, now we celebrate the fruits of our labor. You seem real tense right now. Please chill for a few hours, kid. My word, it'll be well worth it. Let's roll." He pulled the key card to the room out of his side pocket and slid it into the lock of the hotel room. It switched from the color red to green, then clicked open. He smiled at me and pushed it inward. "You good?"

I nodded my head. I'd flipped five cars in one night, was guaranteed to get a nice amount of paper first thing in the morning, I was good to go. I needed to let back for a few hours. I had to get Jade off my mind. She was captivating my every thought and I ain't like that one bit, especially since I knew she wasn't messing with me on that level. Though I think that was the most intriguing part of it all. "Bruh, I'm good. Let's kick back for old times' sake. Payday is in the morning, right?"

He opened the door all the way up and a rush of loud and perfume invaded my nostrils, along with the sultry voice of Ella Mai on the hotel's speakers coming out the room we were set to enter. "Yeah, we get them Benjamins in the morning, but tonight, it's all about pussy." He stepped inside and moved out the way.

Keri was just stepping out of the bathroom. She looked, saw me, and smiled. Her long curly hair was drooped down her back. Her golden skin glistened in the light. She wore a tight Fendi dress that clung to her curves. Her backside poked out the back of her dress as if it was fake or somethin'. Her double-D breasts poked against her top, the nipples visible. She held a bottle of Moët in one hand, and her cell phone in the other. "Papi, oh my God, it's about time you got here. I was almost ready to leave." She rushed over to me and wrapped her arms around my neck. I could feel her breasts pressed up against my chest. They made me feel some type of way. It had been a short minute since she and I had connected, and I was feening for some of that pussy. I hugged her body and slid my hands down and cuffed her ass, roamed under her skirt, so I could feel bare hot cheeks. She wore a G-string that served very little purpose in covering her derriere.

Keri was something like my girlfriend, without the title. In my opinion, we were pretty much fuck buddies. Whenever I wanted some, I'd hit her up because she was an animal in the sack, and she loved to talk that Spanish shit while we did our thing. She and I had been messing around ever since the tenth grade, when we both attended Malcolm X High. We dated off and on, but there were never any strings attached, at least not on my end.

"Papi, tell me we're about to do our thing? I been waiting on you all day." She eased her face into the crook of my neck, smelled me, then licked along the thick vein on the left side, before biting into me and moaning all sexy-like.

I slipped the band of her G-string to the side and played with her lips. I searched through them until I found her clit, pinched it, and rotated my finger all around it, until it became slippery. "Yo, we about to get lit, ma. I'ma watch you dance for me, and then I'ma slay that pussy. You wit that?" My finger entered her box. I slid it all the way into her until it rested against my knuckle. Her box felt hot and swampy. I couldn't wait to get in between those thighs.

There was another Puerto Rican girl that ran past Keri and into Santana's arms. She was about five feet even, with short curly hair and had the body of a money-making stripper. I nonchalantly peeped her ass as she hugged him. It was poked out like the back of a Buick. "Hey, baby. I brought Mollie. I got Percs. And, of course, I brought me. We're about to have a good time." She stepped on her tippy toes and kissed his lips. He palmed her ass, and tongued her down, then opened his mouth and allowed her to drop two pills on his tongue.

Keri looked up at me with her brown eyes. "Damn, papi, you see somethin' over there you like?" Her forehead wrinkled in irritation.

"Yeah, shorty got a fat lil ass on her. I was peeping that shit."

Santana's plaything looked over her shoulder at me. "Unfortunately, you gon have to settle for Keri, unless Santana tryna get down like that tonight. If he wit it, then I'm wit it. But, if he ain't, then it's all bad for you, homeboy." She turned back to him and kissed his lips.

"Yo, what's her name, Santana?" I asked, still peeping that fat booty. Her frame was little, but that derriere was righteous. I couldn't stop looking at it.

"Milan. And her head game is colder than Mount Everest, kid, my word. If Keri a' let you test drive her, we can swap it out for the night. I been wanting to see what's good wit Keri for years anyway." He licked his lips and looked down at her.

Keri shook her head. "This ain't that type of party. Besides, that bitch ain't all that anyway. Anything she can do, I can do better. Bentley, you know what it is. This Brooklyn right here." She cuffed my piece through my pants and pulled me to follow her into the area of the Hilton where

107

there was a long white leather couch, and a love seat right across from it. I sat down and she stepped away and turned on Nicki Minaj's, "Chun Li" track. Came back and stood in front of me, slowly moving her hips to the music while across the room, Milan got ready to dance for Santana as well, clothed in a tight skirt dress that showed off her slopes and curves. Santana yanked her skirt upward to expose that she was naked underneath. Her golden cheeks jiggled. She spread her legs slightly, and I was able to make out the flower between her legs. It was shaven and plump.

Keri grabbed my face and made me look directly up to her. Frowning, she raised her own skirt above her hips while dancing in a suggestive manner. She dropped the skirt and stepped out of it. She stood before me in the small G-string that clung to the folds of her sex lips, so much so that I could make out the slit between them. "Look at me, papi, you see how thick I'm getting?" She slid her fingers into her middle and squeezed her mound. The nipples on her breasts were fully erect.

I ran my hands up and down her thighs, then in between them. Played with her camel toe, and felt the heat coming from it. "Yo, give me a lap dance, ma. Better than you be doing for them niggas in the club too." I turned her around and made her sit my lap. Her long hair flapped into my face. It smelled like cherries. I reached around and took a hold of her breasts, trapped the nipples with my fingertips, pulling on them.

"Ooo, papi, you're making me wet, I just want you to fuck me so bad." She arched her back, and slowly began to dance in my lap, rotating her hips and moaning deep in her throat. I pulled her blouse up over her breasts. She was without a bra. The big globes felt hot in my hands, like hot water balloons. The hard nipples poked at my hands. I looked across the room. Milan turned her back to Santana, grinding in his lap. She stood up and hiked her skirt all the way up and opened her thighs wide, showing me her valley. Placed her hand in her lap and spread the lips so I could see her pink wink, and blew me a kiss.

This made my piece jerk under Keri. "Yo, suck me, Keri. Hurry up, ma." I pushed her off my lap and to the floor. She fell on her knees and yelped in pain, landing on one of her red-bottomed high heels. I didn't give no fucks. I needed to be in her mouth already.

"Damn, papi, you handling me kind of rough, ain't you?" She pulled my jeans down and fished my dick out, getting her mouth wet, stroking my already hard member up and down.

I guided her face forward. She was blocking my way from seeing Milan. After she moved, I was able to see her fingering her pussy. The thick lips were slayed wide. Juices poured out of her crease. The sight drove me nuts. Keri sucked me hard, and ran her hand up under my shirt and over the ripples of my abs. Her jaws hollowed in and out, then she would pop me out, only lick all over me. It felt so good that I started to breathe heavy. Across the way, Milan slid a condom onto Santana's dick and straddled his lap, eased down onto it with her back to me. She grabbed the top of the couch for leverage and got to riding him fast, while he dug his fingers into the flesh of her ass. She looked over her shoulder at me, made eye contact, flicked her tongue and winced in pain while she rode him. "Uh shit. Shit. This dick feel so good, Santana. Fuck, this dick feel so good." Her voice sounded strained.

Keri stood up and rushed to her purse, took out a Magnum and ripped it open. Put it in her mouth and knelt in front of me again. Rolled the condom onto my piece in one fluid motion, then straddled me and mixed all over my lips. "Fuck that bitch, papi. You know I got that fye." Her eyes rolled into the back of her head as she eased onto my dick. Sunk all the way down, then slowly rose to her tippy toes, before sliding down again. Then, she was bouncing up and down on my wood, sucking on my neck "Aw, shit. Aw shit. Aw shit. Aw shit, papi. Papi, aw, papi."

I grabbed her hips, rose from the couch to meet each one of her landings with an upward thrust burying my dick into the deepest regions of her womb. Her titties bounced up and down under my chin. I grabbed them and pushed them together, sucking the nipples while she rode me, moaning loudly.

Across the way, Santana bent Milan over the arm of the couch and got to fucking her so hard that tears were coming out of her eyes. "Yes. Yes. Yes. Ay. Fuck me. Fuck me. Oh-shit!" She slammed back into his lap harder and harder. Her big breasts danced about on her chest. Her hair fell all over her face. Hiding it from my view.

Keri tensed up, grabbed the back of my neck, and screamed into my jaw, cumming hard. I could feel her walls sucking at me, vibrating like a cell phone. "Un. Un. Un. Shit! Papi!" She bounced higher and higher, before sliding off of me, and bending over the table with her ass in the air. She played between her legs and opened the lips for me to see. "Come on, papi, hit this shit. Don't let them show us up," she moaned, spreading her feet apart.

I stroked my dick and got behind her. Rubbed up and down her slit, opened her garden before slowly sliding into her, then ramming home.

"Uh! Bentley! Fuckin' Bentley! Hit this shit, papi. That bitch ain't got shit on me. Fuck me harder than he fuckin' her. Kill my pussy! Kill it, papi."

I got to killing that shit. Low key, I was competing wit Santana, but I also was imagining that I was fucking Milan too. Keri was bad and all that, but I'd already had her before, whereas Milan would have been new pussy and for me, there was nothing more exciting than new money and new pussy. I grabbed a handful of her hair and long-stroked that valley from the back as hard as I could. She got to screaming and slamming back into me. Arching her back and begging me to slow down.

Santana pulled out of Milan and picked her lil ass up and got to fucking her in the air. Bouncing her up and down like a sex doll. She threw her head back. "That's why I love fucking the niggas. Aw shit. Only black dick a' do! Uh, I'm cumming nig-ga!" she hollered.

I turned Keri around and fell to the floor wit her, threw her legs on my shoulder blades and forced her into a ball. Once there, my long stroke game went into full effect. She opened her mouth wide and started whimpering, "Please, Bentley. Please. Aw, papi. You killing me. Un. Un. Uh! You killing me! Shit!"

Bam. Twkk. Bam. Twkk. Bam. Twkk. Bam. Twkk. Bam. Twkk. Bam. Twkk.

I ran in and out of her faster and faster with no mercy, rolled my back, and pulled her to me aggressively. "Gimme this pussy, bitch! Give it to me! Beg me to cum in this shit! Beg me!" I growled going to town on that cat.

"Uh! Cum in me! Cum in me! Aw fuck, Bentley, you killing me!"

I pounded into her with ten long strokes and came hard, biting into her neck, jerking with each release of my seed. I remained planted in her for a full minute, before dislodging. As I was doing so, I looked over to see Milan and Santana watching us. Milan rubbed her box and looked down at my pole. "Dang, Santana, I wanna see what ya mans like." She slid her fingers deep into her mound and pulled them out, sucking them into her mouth.

"Yo, I'm wit the swap. His bitch tripping though."

Keri got up from the floor, and pulled her skirt down. "I'm just fuckin' wit Bentley. He my nigga, y'all gotta respect that."

I stood up and pulled off the rubber, my piece throbbed up and down as I tied it into a knot. "Yo shorty, stop acting like you got papers on me. If I wanna fuck that bitch, I will. You gon either get down or get yo ass out. You know what it is." I hated when a female tried to stake a claim on me like I was a piece of property or something. I wasn't wit that shit at all. Keri had that real bad. Her way of fending off other females was to make it seem like we were more than we was. In my eyes, she was just pussy. There was no depth to her.

"Dang, Bentley, you gon talk to me like that? I thought we better than that." She fixed her top and flipped her hair over her shoulders.

"Nah, I just don't like when you try and stake a claim to me and shit. We cool lil one, but I do what I wanna do, get that shit straight." I mugged her, getting more heated than I meant to.

"I'm sorry. I ain't mean it like that. I thought I was holding you down. I guess I'll just keep my comments to myself. Excuse me." She started to get dressed.

Milan walked over to me and took ahold of my piece, stroking it up and down. "She seem too uptight to me. It ain't nothin' but sex, damn." She got down on her knees, kissed the head, then sucked me into her mouth with her eyes closed.

Keri watched for a second, shook her head and ran out of the room. "You know how I feel about you, Bentley. You just know." She ran into the bathroom and closed the door. I could hear her cursing me out.

Santana walked over and knocked on the door. Every few seconds, he'd look over his shoulder to see what Milan was doing to me. "Yo Keri, open up, let me holler at you right quick."

"I don't feel like talking, Santana. I'm pissed off. That nigga bogus. He been jocking that punk bitch since he first laid eyes on her. I hope you know she do that to every nigga she think is hot, even at our club!" she screamed through the door.

Milan popped my dick out of her mouth. "Damn, bitch, quit hating!" she snapped.

Hearing what Keri said threw me off just a bit. She tried to slide me back into her mouth, but I smacked my hand against her forehead and pushed her back. "Yo, you trifling like that? Get off of me, Yo head game ain't all what bruh said it was anyway." I brushed past her.

"Wait, Bentley. I was just getting started. You gotta let me get into it, then I'ma change yo life." She said this, sashaying across the floor on her knees.

I moved Santana out of the way, and twisted the knob on the bathroom door, finding it locked. "Bruh, tell that bitch to get up, she embarrassing herself. I ain't fuckin wit her on the level. I'm good." I beat on the bathroom door. "Keri, open the door, it's the god."

I heard it click. I twisted the knob, stepped inside, and closed it back. Grabbed a towel that was hanging on the rack, and soaped it up, dropping my pants. "Why you in here acting all out of yo body for? I thought you was a boss, shorty?" I filled the sink to the brim, then dropped my piece inside of it, taking a nice ho bath.

"I am a boss. I just don't like how you played me out there. You don't even know her and she making you front on me. That ain't cool. I thought you had more respect for me than that, that's all." She sat on the rim of the tub and watched me get right.

"I got mad respect for you, Keri, but I ain't yo nigga though. Every time it's another bad bitch in the room, you get intimidated and get to making it seem like you're my woman, when you ain't."

She stood up. "Why ain't I, Bentley? We been fucking round since the tenth grade. You the only man I know the way I do. I been ready to make us official, you been the one that been tripping, for the record."

I rinsed my manhood and dried him off, popped him back into my pants, and situated my clothes. "I ain't ready to be held down by no female. I ain't got my shit together, and I got more stuff on my plate than a fat nigga at a buffet. I gotta get my moms right, myself, and a whole other list of things, before I can even begin to wrap my head around a relationship. Besides, you ain't grinding wit me, shorty. You ain't walking side by side with me. You don't understand my struggle, so for those reasons, you ain't fit to be nothing more than some pussy I hit from time to time. You don't even know what you wanna do wit your life, do you?"

She rolled her eyes. "Here we go wit this shit again. Look, I'm only eighteen. I ain't thinking about the future yet. Right now I'm just stripping, making my money, and having fun. I got plenty of time to figure all that other stuff out. If you ain't fuckin' wit me right now, it's good. I ain't gon keep sweating yo ass. Life goes on. You ain't all that anyway, you just know how to fuck, that's about it." She grabbed her purse off the vanity and reached for the doorknob, stopped and took a deep breath. "I guess I'll see you in a few days or whenever you wanna get back up wit me, huh?"

"Unless you about to tell me how you gon help me advance out here in these streets, we ain't got shit else to talk about. I done already fucked, so..." I rinsed out the towel again and turned my back on her.

She opened the door, and stepped halfway out of it, stopped, and tilted her head back. Exhaled loudly, and came back into the bathroom and closed the door. "Bentley, you the only nigga that do me like this. Damn, you hurting my feelings. What can I do, baby? Please, I'll do anything," she whined.

As bad as Keri was, deep down, she was soft. She ain't really have no self-esteem or self-worth. She was used to niggas fawning all over her because of her beauty, but I never had. I knew the key to controlling her lie in how I treated her. For me, the harder a female was, the more I made it seem like I didn't give a fuck about them. They were accustomed to the world kissing their ass, so when that didn't happen it made their system overload. She was no different. It was Friday night, so her club had to have been jumping for the last three days. I needed some of that paper, that's my angle. And, before I could bring that up, she reached into her Fendi purse, and pulled out a knot of cash. "Look, I don't know how much it is, but it's yours. Just take it, and treat me better, please, papi." She handed it to me and wrapped her arms around my neck, holding me tight.

I smiled, slid my hands around and cuffed that ass. "I can only be me, ma, I ain't about to change for nobody. I can't turn this shit off. You gotta step yo game up. I know my worth."

"Okay, papi. Okay."

T.J. & Jelissa

Chapter 10

Bentley

Instead of us getting our money the first thing in the morning, the British dude gave Santana the run-around until about two that afternoon. He had us meet up with one of his contacts, where we were paid fifty gees total. Santana bussed it down the middle with me, and we shook up. "Yo kid, I got another kick lined up for us in about three days. Until then, I'ma go fuck wit my baby mother out in Jersey. She been hassling me about seeing my daughter, so I'ma go handle my manly bidness. I'ma fuck wit you after I get back, it's all love." He gave me a hug, and stepped back. Yo, shorty been blowing up the phone too. I was gon tell you, but while we was trying to lock down this money, I ain't wanna tie the lines up." He showed me eight text messages that Jade had sent, and four missed calls. "Yo, that bitch sweating you already," he snickered.

I cringed as soon as the bitch word came out of his mouth in regards to her. I don't know why, but I did. I snatched the phone out of his hand, and sent her a text, letting her know that I was on my way. Eyed him angrily, and clenched my jaw. "I left her in a trap, with no electricity, or gas, Blood. I was bogus. Anything could've happened to her, and you couldn't tell me she reached out to you! My word, I should steal you." I opened the driver's door and got in the truck he was rolling. "Let's go."

He mugged me for a long time, then walked around the truck, and got in and slammed the door. "Bruh, why you bugging? You got somethin' going wit this bitch a somethin?"

I peeled out the alley, and got right onto the expressway. The sun was shining bright. It felt at least seventy degrees out. The breeze was nice. It looked like it was going to be a good day. "Yo, I just gotta look out for her right now, that's all. I shouldn't have left her alone all night. That's a fuckin trap house. Ain't no telling why she was getting at your phone back-to-back like that. I feel like shit."

Santana scoffed. "Nigga, it's money over bitches. You was out chasing money. She ain't out doing shit, so it is what it is. She a be aiight, word up."

I looked over at him and bit my tongue. I couldn't knock him for feeling how he felt, so I just kept my mouth closed. "Good looking on the lick, bruh. I ain't mean to get down on you like I did. I'm just gon handle my bidness wit her and get at you in a few days. It's good, B."

Instead of saying another word, he turned up *Tha Carter V*, and pulled out a blunt, sparking it and taking deep tokes of the URB.

***

It took me twenty minutes to get to Harlem. When I got there, I grabbed the book bag full of cash off the backseat, and ran up the steps to Santana's trap, got into the hallway, and ran up the stairs as fast as I could. I slid the key into the lock, and twisted it.

Jade was fifteen feet away from the door, knelt in front of the couch, with the same sheet wrapped around her shoulders. Her hair was brushed backward into a ponytail. There were bags under her eyes, and she looked a bit sick. She looked slimmer than when I'd first laid eyes on her. She looked up to me, and a tear dropped from her left eye. I closed the door and rushed over to her, knelt in front of her, looking her over closely. "Jade? What's the matter? Did somebody hurt you? Talk to me?" I was feeling guilty. I knew I was bogus for leaving her in a trap house all night while I fucked off with Keri. Man, I felt like shit. I was praying nothing had happened to her. She had the shades drawn, so it looked dark inside the apartment. I reached out my hand to touch her face, and couldn't believe that she allowed me to. More tears fell from her eyes. "What's the matter?"

"Before I tell you what I just found out, I want to share somethin' with you that I've never shared with anyone. I don't know why I'm doing this, but please don't judge me." She sniffled, and wiped her nose, then slowly turned away from me. Pulled the sheet forward, and exposed her naked back. It was full of small burn marks. There had to be at least eighty of them, if not more.

I felt a wave of emotions rush through me. My eyes watered, and I got angry at the same time, already coming to a conclusion of whom the culprit might have been. "Jade." I dared to extend my fingers to her scars, touched the rough pieces of scar tissue. "What happened?"

"It started when I was three years old. Back when my parents first moved to Brooklyn from Jersey. Things were real rough, and my father had to work two jobs, just to make ends meet. Around this time, he and my mother started to have a lot of arguments and that led to the fights, which led to my father kicking my mother out of the one bedroom we had in our apartment. He'd kick her out, but would allow me to sleep in there with him. He made a habit of telling her that if I had not been born, he would have kicked her to the curb a long time ago. That he didn't love her, that he only loved me, his princess." She began to cry harder. Her shoulders were slumped. As she cried, her shoulders bounced up and

119

down a tad. The sheet had come off enough for me to see the side swells of her breasts, but I did not sexualize them in this moment, could not. I was feeling her pain and needed to go there with her.

I rubbed over her scars. "Go ahead, Jade. I'm listening."

She sniffed and wiped her nose again. Shook her head. "My mother hated when he said those things. Hated when he told her how much he loved me and hated her. Disliked the relationship that I had with my father, so out of hatred for him and jealousy for me, nearly every night she would put her cigarettes out on my back whenever he was not around. Then, when I started to cry from the pain, she would beat me until I couldn't cry no more. Throw me in a scalding hot bath and leave me there until it cooled, then off to bed I went." She dropped her had to the carpet. "All I ever wanted was for my mother to love me. I didn't ask to be brought into this world. I didn't ask for my father to treat her the way he did." She rocked back and forth on her haunches. The sheet fell around her. Her hands were in front of her face, covering it. She lowered her face all the way to the carpet, and turned it sideways with her eyes closed. "My mother beat me every single day and every single night, for the things my father put her through, and when she got tired of beating me, she turned on my sisters. Their backs reflect the picture of mine. No matter how much I tried to shield those girls, I could never protect them. I hate me."

I crawled closer to her and pulled the sheet up around her, wrapped it as best as I could, pulled her up and laid her head on my chest. "Jade, I swear, I'll never let nobody hurt you again. You've been through a lot, ma, but no more. I swear, no more." I could only imagine the pain she was feeling. I honestly didn't know what to say. I just knew I needed to be there for her to hear her out. "Is there anything I can do to make you feel better?"

She swallowed and looked up at me. "You asked me what happened to my back, and I just wanted you to know. On top of that, my mother tried to kill herself at the county jail yesterday. I called and acted as if I was my aunt Sondra over in Jersey, and that's how I found out. She slit her wrists. She's in the hospital in the intensive care unit. I don't know what to do. I think I want to go and see her." She pulled back and looked up at me again. "Is that stupid?"

I didn't know what to say. After the story she'd just told me, and knowing her mother was in the process of trying to get her charged with her father's murder, I didn't understand how she could have any love for her at all. But, I'd only been given a glimpse of her story. I didn't know it all, so I was in no position to judge her at all. "Jade, right now you and I are both on the run from the law. We can't risk them catching us. If they catch you, more specifically, you're on the ropes for a murder wrap. I know you're innocent, but it would be your mother's words against your own. That's a fifty percent chance you will prevail, and a fifty percent chance you won't. Do you like those odds?"

She came from under me and stood up, shrugging her shoulders. "My whole life, the odds have been against me. I don't fear the odds, I only fear God. I want to see my mother. I need to before I self-destruct." She turned her back to me.

I got to my feet and came up behind her. "Jade, I don't think that would be a good idea. Not right now. I think we should get ourselves together, and then try and buss a move so we can see her, and maybe even your sisters. But, we have to have a plan in place. We can't wing it, that's dangerous."

She faced me and looked into my eyes. "Why did you leave me here all night by myself? Do you know that more than ten of those dope addicts knocked on the door, looking for product? One of them beat on the back window, even after I told him that we didn't have anything. He broke the back window. I was scared for my life." Instead of answering her question, I picked up the book bag, and knelt down in front of her. Unzipped it and pulled out a bundle of money. "This twenty-five racks in here. This should help us to get a safe distance from New York. I'll buss other moves, but for now, this is what we're working wit. This is the reason I stayed out all night. But, I am sorry."

She looked down at me for a moment, then shook her head. "Now that you've seen my whole back, I suppose you're disgusted. It's only a matter of time before you kick me to the curb, huh?"

I stood up. "Jade, I'm fuckin' wit you the long way. Those scars ain't gon detour me from having your back. Ain't neither one of us perfect, and we never will be. You gon see I ain't one of those fuck niggas out there. My loyalty is one hunnit. I know you've been through a lot, and I just want to protect you from going through anything else. Don't ask me why, because I can't tell you why. I just wanna hold you down. I think I like you or somethin'." I smiled as if it were a joke, but I knew I was serious.

She looked at the carpet, then over my shoulder. "Well, I need some new clothes and shoes. I feel so grungy and dirty. Why don't you get me right, and I'll think about what we can do about that crush you got on me." She smirked and walked into the bathroom. "For the record, you smell like perfume, Bentley, got passion marks all on your neck. Chasing money ain't the only thing you did last night." She closed the bathroom door.

My eyes bugged out of my head. I wanted to holler and explain myself, but instead, I remained silent, shaking my

122

head in infatuation. I had to have Jade. I don't know why, but I just did.

***

Jade

I nodded my head with a big smile on my face. Twirled in a circle and looked over the Prada dress in the full-length mirror Bentley insisted on buying for me. Black and purple, with small specks of yellow in it, the price tag was fifteen hundred dollars. I thought he was out of his mind. For that amount, we could have bought me twenty outfits from Walmart, though I had to admit it did look hella good on my frame. "Bentley, it looks good, but fifteen hundred dollars is ridiculous."

He shook his head and got up from the chair he'd been sitting back in, watching me try on one dress after the next in Macy's, until he'd gotten up and picked one out for me. I'd been timid, because the sticker price of every dress I grabbed to try on had been more than a rent payment.

"Yo, don't worry about the price, ma, I got this. When you're as bad as you are, you gotta have your wardrobe all the way up top. Let me handle my bidness. I won't fail you." His eyes met mine in the mirror. "Do you like it?"

I diverted my eyes from his, feeling shy all of a sudden. I prayed he wasn't taking pity on me because of the scars on my back. I was trying my best to push those thoughts out of my mind. I hadn't exposed a bit of my past to receive his sympathy. I didn't need anybody's. "I love it. It would be one of the nicest things I've ever owned."

He smiled. "Then that's all that matters. We gon snatch you up three of these, then a bunch of other less costly ones.

We gotta get yo shoe game up to par too, underthings, and whatever else you need. I'ma blow most of this bag on you, then hit my mom's bills, and get me a few things. We should still have enough to make that transition to Jersey, now are you sure we can trust your aunt?" He stepped behind me, so close I could smell his cologne. It intoxicated me and made me feel uncomfortable at the same time.

I eased back into the dressing room and dropped the dress from my body. Picked it up and put it back on the hanger it had come with, before getting dressed. "My aunt Sondra is cool. She's very understanding, and has been my best friend ever since I was eleven. She went through the some of the same things with her parents as I did with my own. She's just a few years older than us." I grabbed the dress, along with my other things and stepped back into the store where he was.

He had three other dresses in his hand from the Prada collection. He handed them to me, and pulled out a knot of hundreds. "We should be good."

"Yeah, but before we roll out that way, I wanna chill with you tonight. The electricity and gas is turned on, so I was thinking we kick back and watch a few movies and continue to get to know each other. We're about to embark on a crazy journey and I think it'll be smart for each of us to know who the other person really is. Wouldn't you agree?"

It didn't bother me. I was simply happy we wouldn't be forced to sit around in the dark, and there was actually gas now. Thoughts of my mother's situation continued to play on in my mind, but I was really trying my best to not dwell on it. I just wanted to be happy for a night. There had been so many nights of pain. I wanted this night to be different. Even though I wasn't sold on trusting Bentley and I expected for his true nature to rear its ugly head, I wanted to at least give him a chance at friendship. "That's cool wit me. Can I pick the movie?" I asked, carrying all of my things to the counter for him to cash me out. This was my first time having any man spend any amount of money on me. To say that it didn't make me feel like a princess would have been a lie. I looked him over while he licked his thumb and counted off hundreds like a boss. He was fitted in a black and red Marc Jacobs 'fit, with the matching Jordan's. He had on a Bulls fitted cap that set his attire off. He looked real handsome. I'd always had a thing for men that knew how to dress, he was no different.

"It's your world tonight, Jade, whatever you wanna watch is cool, long as I can put my arm around you while we watching it." He smiled and looked back at me.

I was mugging him like he was crazy, even though the notion wasn't that off base. But, I couldn't help but to wonder what he had in mind. I knew he knew that I was on my cycle so I couldn't imagine him thinking sex. I was a bit worried, but I didn't want to allow my paranoia to over whelm me. "Long as you behave, that's cool."

The white female cashier gave him the receipt and smiled at me. "Thank you for shopping at Macy's, you two have a nice day." She flipped her blonde hair over her shoulders and motioned for the next customer to come forward. Checked Bentley out from the corners of her eyes, and licked her lips. I peeped her antics and got irritated. I knew if I hadn't been standing there, she would have tried her luck with him. She been giving him the eye the entire time we'd been in the store from what I saw. I wanted to say something so bad.

Bentley must've seen that because he looked me over, then glanced at her. She smiled, and this made him frown. He slid over to me and put his arm around my neck. "Come on, baby, let me spend some more of this cash on you at

another store. Today, it's all about you, the queen, word up."
He mugged her and we cruised out of the store with me
trying my best to not break into a smile. I knew I wasn't his
woman, but it still felt good to have him flex on another
female with me, checking shit in. I felt honored.

***

He brought the gyro meals out of the kitchen, and set
them on the table in front of the television he'd put up on the
wall. I didn't know where it had come from, but I was glad it
was there. I had the movie paused. He handed me my food
on a plate, and poured me a glass of grape soda, before
settling in beside me. "So, what we watching?" he asked,
peeling back the wrapper to my food first, and then his own.

"*Diary of a Mad Black Woman.*" I laughed, and situated
my food on my lap. It smelled so good, my stomach got to
growling. I fixed the meat in the pita bread, trying my best
not to get my freshly manicured nails all messy. Bentley had
been a gem and taken me to get my hair, nails, and toes
done. He had me feeling so beautiful, I was borderline
emotional.

"Aw man, are you serious?" He looked up at the screen
then over to me, sourly.

"Sure am." I laughed and started the movie. "You said I
could pick any movie that I wanted to, well, I'm picking this
one."

"That's the last thing I need. A movie to give you more
fuel to hate me, when I'm trying so hard for you to see me in
a different light. Damn."

I was about to bite my sandwich but stopped in midair.
"Bentley, I don't hate you. I don't hate anybody, and I am
very thankful for everything you've done for me today. I am

126

trying to see you for who you are, it'll just take a little time. Don't count it out. Please."

He brushed the hair that fell along my shoulder out of the way, and nodded. "Aiight, long as you giving me a chance, I'm cool wit that." He smiled. "Yo, you looking super fine too, Jade. I ain't coming at you or nothin', but I just had to let that be known, word up."

I blushed and grabbed the remote. "Boy, let's watch the movie." I didn't know what to say besides that. Bentley was always flirting wit me and making me feel some type of way. It didn't help that he was so handsome and had this swagger about himself that captivated me. It would have made things so much easier if I could have taken a journey through his mind, so I could know what he really felt and thought about me. I didn't like feeling like a charity case.

"Yo, that's all you gon say? I can't get a thank you or nothing else?" He looked offended.

"Thank you, Bentley. Now can we watch the movie?"

He sat there and looked me over, then set his plate on the table in front of us. "I got a confession, and I don't want you to be mad."

My heart skipped a beat. "What is the confession?" I didn't know what I expected, but I prepared for the worst. I just knew this day couldn't remain perfect. It was the story of my life.

"Jade, I really don't wanna watch this movie. I kinda wanna get to know you. I mean, a movie is meant to bond and pass time with, but we don't really know how much more time we have with each other. Our time could be up in ten minutes, or ten years. Either way, I'm interested in you." He knelt on the floor beside my feet, and looked up at me.

"Are you mad at me?" His hand rested on my knee and gave me tingles. I'd never been alone and in close quarters with a man before. I felt both scared and a bit detoured.

I shook my head. "Nall, I ain't mad at you. I thank you for being honest." I held up my plate. "I am hungry though. We haven't eaten anything all day, so do you think we can feed our faces, then get to know each other a little better?"

He smiled. "Yo, that sound like a plan. I can respect that. I guess we can watch the movie until then, huh?" He got up and sat back next to me. Grabbed his food off the table, and placed it on his lap, opening the pita bread and taking a piece of meat and putting it inside his mouth.

"Look, I know yo don't wanna watch this movie and all that, but we are. You said I could pick any movie I wanted to, and I pick this one. Buckle up." I laughed, grabbed the remote, and started the flick. I glanced over at him, and he smiled at me, his brown eyes seeming to peer into the depths of my soul. For as long as I had been alive, no one had looked at me with such care. "What?" I felt so nervous and jittery all of a sudden.

He shook his head. "Nothin', I'm just looking at you, that's all. Yo Jade, even though our circumstances are a bit tight right now, I'm glad you're here wit me. You look super good too. I just had to say that again." He avoided my eye contact, and looked toward the big screen. "Aiight, we can watch the movie now."

I smiled, and placed a tuft of hair behind my right ear lobe and nodded. "Yeah, let's watch the movie."

Chapter 11

Jade

Bentley lit the last candle on the table, got up and turned all of the lights off inside the house, before coming back and sitting across from me. There was a tub of vanilla ice cream in the middle of us with two plastic sporks inside of it. I didn't know what he had in mind, but he'd been a champ and sat through the entire Tyler Perry movie without getting up one time. I didn't know many dudes that could do that. A part of me wanted to think he'd made the sacrifice for me, but I didn't want to look too far into it.

He took his spork and scooped a bit of ice cream into his mouth. "Aiight, I want to know all about you, and I'm going to open up the floor, so you can ask me anything that you want to."

I smiled. "Anything? And you're going to be one hundred percent honest with me, no matter what I ask?" I needed that stipulation right away, because I had some things that I needed to know before I could cruise down the highway of trusting him.

"Hand to my mother, anything you wanna know I'ma tell you, and I'ma keep that shit one hunnit. I ain't got nothing to hide."

"Okay, well I'm goin' in. When you left me here the other night—"

"Aw shit, here we go," he interrupted me.

"Nall, don't interrupt." I rolled my eyes, but being that we were sitting by candlelight, I don't think that he could see the gesture. "Anyway, when you left me here alone the other night were you with a female? And, by with I mean, did y'all smash? The truth, Bentley."

129

He ran his hand over the top of his waves. "Damn." He sat back in his seat after sticking his spork into the ice cream. "Ma, I'ma keep shit real. Yeah, I was with this lil jump-off. After me and Santana got done handling our bidness, he wanted to celebrate and I did too. Keri and a lil bitch named Milan was already at the Hilton, so me and the homie rolled through there and went to work. It ain't mean shit, but it did happen. I'm sorry."

I felt like he'd slapped me across the face, at the same time trying to console me. I imagined him cooped up in the warm Hilton, smoking and screwing another female while I sat in the cold, dark trap house, sick wit cramps and bloating, while awaiting his return. I wanted to reach across the table and smack him, but I played it cool. "Apology accepted. Thank you for being honest," were the words that came out of my mouth but inside, my blood was boiling. "Okay, your turn."

"Man, I feel like shit now. I really am sorry, Jade, nothin' like that will ever happen again. I was stupid and didn't think things through as clear as I should have. I'll never leave you in the trenches like that again. That's my word."

I nodded. "Bentley, it's fine. We're just getting to know one another. Calm down." I reached across the table and touched his big hand. He appeared to be shaking. I could sense he was deeply affected by his revelations. It made me feel some type of way. Like, he was actually remorseful. Remorseful because he'd hurt me. No one had ever cared about me enough to empathize with the way they'd hurt me. I didn't know how to feel about this. I was confused. "Please, ask me your question?"

He remained silent for a short time, then cleared his throat. "Aiight, what is it going to take for you to trust me? And, do I stand any chance with you?"

I had not been expecting that question. I released my fingers from his skin, and sat back in my chair and shrugged my shoulders. "I don't know, Bentley. I've been through so much. All I know is pain. To trust you would be to set myself up for more of it, when I am so tired of being pain's doorstep. So, I honestly don't know. So far, you've been pretty amazing, I mean with the exception of the other night. No one has ever done the things for me you have, and I am so thankful for them, so maybe remaining consistent is the route to go. Consistency and kindness are foreign topics to me. As far as if you have a chance with me?" I nodded. "I'm broken. Alone, and weary. If you want to put in the work to help me to get to that stage, then yes, yes you do. But my question to you is why would you want to? You're a very good-looking man. I've seen how women flock to you in the projects on the few times that I've passed you by. Even at school you were the topic of conversation in the bathroom, and the female locker room. Due to the fact that you're a hustler, you can have your pick of the litter, so why me?" I leaned forward and gazed into his brown eyes. The flickering of the candles around us caused them to shimmer. His thick eyebrows accentuated the almond shapes that held the windows to his soul.

"Jade, I don't have the right answer. Like, it would be easy for me if I could sit here and run all type of game on you and shit, but I promised to keep it one hunnit, so I can't even do that."

"Bentley, all I want is the truth. Anytime you and I communicate, that's all I'll ever need. Please. Just speak from that true space in your soul and that'll be enough for me."

He nodded and lowered his head. "Jade, I like pussy."

I jerked my head back, taken off guard. "Excuse me?"

"Nall, let me finish." He exhaled loudly and ran his hand over his deep ocean waves again. "I like pussy and for as long as I have, I been shooting to get the baddest bitches that cross my path so I could slay 'em. Me and the homie Santana. But for me, I've always needed more than just a pretty face. I needed a female to make me feel something. To buss moves for me, and accommodate me when it comes to this street life. I've been a taker ever since I could remember, because my heart is so cold. But then, when I ran into ya moms on the stairwell, and found out what had taken place with her and who had done it, then saw the way ya old man had did a number on you, that shit made me angry. Had blood been alive, I think I would have smoked him just on the strength of how he did you queens."

"Oh, so this is some charity type stuff? I should have known. Look, I don't need your fuckin' charity or your sympathy, Bentley. In case you haven't noticed, I'm a fighter. You can take pity on somebody else, because I ain't the one." I scooted my chair back and stood up. I didn't know where I was about to go, but I didn't want to be there any longer. I didn't need his fuckin' pity. The thought alone made me sick to my stomach and angry.

He jumped up and took ahold of my wrist. "Jade, this ain't fair. How you gon ask me a question, then not give me the proper chance to answer it? That ain't right. Now, I wasn't done. Sit ya ass down," he ordered, peering into my eyes with an angry scowl on his face.

"Who are you talking to like that?" I yanked my arm away from him.

He held up his hands in retreat. "That's my bad, but please, can you sit down for a second so I can answer this question?"

I pulled the chair from the table and sat in it with my arms crossed. "Go ahead. I'll listen, but I pretty much heard everything I needed to hear already. You see me as a charity case. I just wanna know when this good nature of yours is goin' to wear off? I know it's just a matter of time. I mean, you're already grabbing on me and shit."

He looked at the ceiling and shook his head. "Yo because you got this warped view of me in your head and it's so fuckin' insulting. Damn. You ask me a question, but then you don't give me the space to answer it. That's weak. Then, before I can get my thoughts to flowing on some honest shit, you cut into what I've already said and get to judging me, now I'm second guessing my truths and feel like I'm lying."

I stood up. "Well, we're done here, because I don't want a lie. You swore to tell me the truth. I been lied to enough in my life. I don't need more of the same." I felt my eyes beginning to water because I was getting angry at him, and I didn't want to be in that space. I just wanted to finish the day happy. I'd never had a twenty-four-hour period that was dedicated to me. This had been the first, and though the day had been magical with all of the pampering and shopping, the night was setting up to be a horrible one. I just knew everything had been too good to be true.

He came from around the table and stepped in front of me. Took a mighty hold of my wrists and looked into my eyes. His cologne drifted into my nostrils. He smelled like a man. The height of him towered over me. For the first time, I was fully aware of how big and muscular he actually was. He made me feel small. Like a little girl. "Jade, let me finish with my truth, please." He moved my hair out of my face, and placed it behind my shoulders like he had done before. The gesture was enough to soften me. I hated myself for being low-key sweet on him. Knew that any lowering of my guard could be catastrophic for an already broken me.

"Go ahead, Bentley." I pulled away from him, and sat back in my chair, crossing by legs.

He took the time to walk around the table and seat himself. "Like I was saying, I saw how ya old man did you and your moms, and I ain't like it. Then, after you and I did everything we could to set shit straight, ya moms wind up flipping the script on you. I ain't like that either, so yeah, that made me want to protect you. But, it ain't got nothin' to do wit pity. In addition to all of this, I've always had a small thing for you. I say small because once I found out who your pops was, and how he got down wit them rock heads in our building, every time I saw you after that all I saw were his features in you, and that was a turn off. But still in all, in my opinion, you were the baddest bi..." He caught himself. "Queen in our school. The reason why I want to take the time to get to know you so you can turn into my woman is because we are so much alike, and our stories are similar. You are the female version of me."

"How so?" I asked, barely above a whisper. I needed to see where he was going with things.

"Is that your next question?"

"Yeah, how so?"

"Instead of me telling you, let me just show you." He stood up, and pulled his shirt from over his head, standing before me in a black tank top that made his lean muscles pop. Before I could take the time out to admire them, he pulled the beater over his head. The candlelight made him look like a chocolate god. His stomach muscles were prominent. His abs were perfectly separated. "Yo, you see these two scars right here?" He pointed to two scars that looked to be about three inches long, and an inch in width.

"Yeah I see 'em."

"Back in two thousand and two, when I was two years old, my mother tried to take my life."

I gasped and covered my mouth. "I'm so sorry." My eyes watered. A sole tear slid down each cheek.

"It's okay, Jade, but let me finish."

I nodded. "Go ahead."

"Back then, my pops was a golden-gloved boxer out in Harlem, and he was making crazy bread. He had plenty women flocking to him, and throwing the pussy at him, long story short he got to neglecting my mother real tough. Beating her senseless and all that shit. He even kicked us out of his crib one night two days before Christmas, so he could trick off with a bunch of groupies. This was the night my mother had taken all she could. So, in the alley of one-forty-five Lennox, she stabbed me two times in the chest with a box cutter, and left me for dead. Kicked me into a garage and everything."

Now I was crying like a big baby. "I'm so sorry. How are you still alive?"

Unbeknownst to her, the garage she'd kicked me into was being occupied by a female crack head. She woke up to my crying a short time after and scooped me into her arms. I can still remember the scent of her unwashed body, and the stank of her breath as she rocked me against her and ran into the alley with my bleeding body. She ran screaming for help, and I remember her constantly repeating, she wished she had a car. She wished she had a car. 'Lord, please don't let this baby die, oh I wish I had a car.' She said this over and over while she ran all the way to Mercy Hospital, where they in turn, helped her to save my life. I wound up in foster care for six years. The judge finally released me into my father's care after that time had passed.

My father had retired from boxing and started drinking real heavily. Somehow, he and my mother got back together, and it's never been exposed that she'd been the one that had tried to kill me. To this day, my father thinks she was robbed, and I was harmed in the process. Always thought I would go to the grave with that secret, but I hope it helps you to see where I'm coming from." He came around and knelt on the side of me. "Jade, your scars are my scars. No, I can't take away any of the pain you've experienced, but from here on out, you don't have to be alone. You don't have to look at your scars as ugly. You don't have to feel less than, because to me, you are beautiful."

I shook my head. "Don't say that, Bentley. I'm not beautiful. I'm ugly and I know it. My mother has told me this every single day of my life. It's all I know. It's what I believe to be true."

He wiped away my tears. "No disrespect to your mother, but she lied. You are the most beautiful woman in this whole world, and those scars of pain on your back only solidify this truth. Those scars say you've been through something. They tell a story of a warrior. A goddess. A story that I'd love to read every page of."

I sniffled and shook my head. "Bentley, I'm scared. I'm scared that one day you're going to change your feelings. That you're going to build me all the way up, just to let me down. I'm so fragile, I don't want to go there with you, please don't make me."

He palmed the side of my face. His hand was warm. The fingers slid into my hair. "I won't hurt you, Jade. All I need is a chance. Just give me a chance to at first be a friend you can trust. Let me ride beside you until we figure our situations out, then we'll take it from there. If you don't feel I am worthy to be your man, then we won't go there. But if at the end of it all, I am proven to be who I say I am, then I ask that you give me that shot. I just want to love you, Jade. I want to protect you. I wanna uplift you and in turn, I want you to do the same for me, because like you, I am a broken man. All I know is money and bitches. I need to grasp the concept of stability and a true queen." His thumb caressed my cheek. It felt good. He gazed into my eyes and was silent. "Can you give me a chance?"

I nodded. "Yeah, I can. I mean, I'm not gon lie and say I don't need you, because I do. I'm weak. Your story touched me. I couldn't tell that by just looking at you, and you still talk about your mother like she is the most important person in your life. You're paying all of her bills. I would have never guessed that she tried to kill you when you were younger. We have way more in common than I think I will have with any other man, so yeah, I want us to take the proper steps to become something for each other. I'd like to help you heal. And, I'd love it if you helped me as well." I sniffled again. I could feel a bit of snot sneak out of my left nostril, and before I could maneuver myself to wipe it away with a napkin from the table, Bentley had done so with his thumb. That made me shudder.

He wiped it in the paper towels alongside of the tub of ice cream, then came back and pulled me up. "I'ma do whatever I gotta do to heal you. You're a diamond, Jade. I see it and I wanna cherish you." He snatched me to his body, slightly leaned me backward and kissed my lips with reckless abandon.

I felt tingles shoot all over me. His grip. His scent. The spontaneity. The revelation of our similar stories. I felt the need to be held by him. It all worked out for the greater good of the moment. Though my apprehension of us was there, I allowed myself to melt into the oasis of him.

He sucked all over my lips, moaning into my mouth. My lips attacked back with hunger. My arms tightened around his neck. I surrendered. Sucking and licking his thick lips, until he released me. His chest heaved up and down, he was just as out of breath as I was. "I'm sorry, Jade. I just had to have them lips. I been wanting to kiss you since I first laid eyes on you. Damn, you're becoming too much for me."

I chuckled, looking into his mesmerizing eyes. "I can say the same."

Chapter 12

Bentley

My mother adjusted her weight from one foot unto the next. It was three days later, and I'd agreed to meet her at her friend Bonnie's house out in the Bronx, figuring both me and Jade were too hot to be fucking around in Brooklyn. "Dang, Bentley, you know I don't like when you show up unannounced with people with you. Got me out here looking all scruffy and shit. Damn."

I slid the bag of Mc Donald's across the table, along with her Pepsi soft drink. "Ma, you're good. Jade is more thankful for you having saved her life more than anything else, ain't you, Jade?"

Jade sat close to me on the couch with her legs crossed. She was rocking this Burberry skirt-dress I'd copped for her, pink and black, with the all black and pink Burberry three-inch heels. Her wavy hair fell off her shoulders, and her eyebrows were freshly plucked. No make-up, she was killing me. "Yes, ma'am, I could never judge you. You saved my life and I love you for it. I mean that from the bottom of my heart."

My mother smiled, and ran her fingers through her unkempt hair. There was lint all in it. Her jogging pants were stained, so was the white t-shirt she wore with Kool-Aid all over it. She smelled real bad too. Like seafood and musk. All those things made me sick to my stomach with both emotions and disgust. I sat before a lost woman. "You the lil girl from the other night?" She smacked her lips and took a Newport out the nearly empty pack that sat on the table. Lit it, and blew the smoke toward us.

I fanned it away. "Keep that poison over there, Mama." I hated the smell of cigarette smoke. I never understood why anybody could get addicted to something that couldn't get you high. It seemed pointless to me.

"I'm sorry, baby." She waved the smoke away, and took another pull.

There were roaches crawling all over the walls. The house was dirty and smelled as bad as it looked. All the appliances had been hocked for crack, according to my mother who let it be known every time her and her friend Bonnie got into a fight or major argument.

"Yes, ma'am, I'm the one that you and your son saved. I just wanted to say thank you for that. Had you not been there, only God knows what might've happened to me."

My mother sat her cigarette in the ashtray and pulled a pipe out of her bra, one that was already burnt on the ends. She reached into her jogging pants pocket and came up with a sandwich bag with two rocks inside of it. Took one out, and placed it in the pipe. "Shid, girl, you damn near family then. I can be myself around you." She laughed and lit the rock, pulling on the pipe hard. Her jaws sucked inward. After she cleared the pipe, she got to smacking her lips loudly, and holding the dope smoke in. I was so embarrassed that I wanted to snatch her ass up and shake some common sense into her. But, I allowed her to finish and sat back angrily and impatiently.

Jade took my hand and interlocked her fingers with mine. This was the first time she'd done somethin' like that. I took it as a sign of her understanding that my mother was embarrassing me, and her way of telling me I was okay. Either way, her fingers gave me comfort.

My mother sat her pipe on the table and smiled at me with eyes bucked so big that she looked shocked and caught off guard. "So, what brings you to the Bronx? You know the police looking for you, don't you? Her too. They say she's wanted for murder. Now that I had a good look at her, that's definitely who they been looking for. Got five grand for anybody that give up information of her whereabouts too. They been all over Red Hook."

"Yeah, we know all that. She ain't do what they tryna say she did. I'm a witness to her truth. But, why are you telling me this?"

She grabbed the Pepsi and drank from it. "Just thought you should know. That's all. Why she kill her daddy anyway? Was he touching her?" She picked up the cigarette and relit it.

Jade tensed up and squeezed my hand. I could tell that she wanted to say something, but was biting her tongue on the strength that she was my mother. She turned to me and smiled, then flared her nostrils.

"Ma, I just told you she ain't kill that dude. It's a long story, but it ain't our bidness. I thought you was gon try and kick that nasty habit." I was trying to change the subject, and I wanted to address her crack usage as well. I was starting to think coming over there this day was a huge mistake. I was praying this wouldn't set me and Jade backwards. I felt like I was making a lot of good ground wit her.

She waved me off. "Boy, I don't wanna hear that shit. This candy is all I got in life, especially since you've abandoned me. What made you shoot your daddy's bitch? You finally getting her back from taking his trifling ass away from us? You shoulda kilt her." She giggled, and filled her pipe wit another rock, lit it so fast with the long flame coming out of her lighter, I was unable to stop her. She exhaled thick clouds of smoke out of her nostrils.

141

The smoke smelled like burnt plastic and sugar. It turned my stomach. I'd hated the smell of it ever since my mother began to do the drug.

"Me and Pops got to wrestling. His gun fell and went off. The bullet hit her, it wasn't my fault."

My mother's eyes were really big now. "What the hell are two grown ass men wrestling about? Your father must know that girl like you. I done caught her a couple times lusting after you with her eyes. I wouldn't be surprised if y'all was screwing behind his back. It would serve him right for how he did me. And you for that matter." She scratched her nappy hair and leaned all the way in her chair. I noticed there was cold all in her eyes, and slob crust in the corners of her mouthpiece. She looked real bad. Life had taken a toll on her.

"Me and Pops always arguing and fighting about something. You know that. It ain't no thang. It was just a crazy accident, I don't know why he wiling all of a sudden." I needed to move past this subject before something came out that I didn't want Jade to hear. My mother had a real big mouth, especially when she was on that dope. I already knew how game-conscious Jade was. I felt that the more my mother said, the more it would feed Jade's curiosity. I could see her demanding an explanation later on.

"Yeah well, I saw that girl a few days ago and she damn near broke into tears, saying how much she needed to talk to you. She say you blocked her all over the place, and that she knows it isn't your fault. That your father called the police and she ain't have nothing to do wit it, but they are looking for you, so be careful. She told me to tell you she love you, and she really need to see you. The bitch confided in me like she ain't steal my husband away from me, carrying his child. Her belly all big and shit. I wanted to smack her pretty-ass face after I spit in it. I got a cold too. Her and her unborn would've been just as sick." She laughed and started coughing.

"Mama, I paid up all of your bills, so you're good for another two months. Do you need any household items? Can I take you grocery shopping or anything? Or clothes shopping?"

She shook her head. "Nall baby, all Mama need is some money. You can give me the cash and I'll make it happen for myself. I need to party a lil bit. Get my groove back. It's been a little while since I had it." She laughed at her own joke. "Son, you wanna pay for my trip to Jamaica? I promise to find you a step daddy."

I looked her over and couldn't believe how far she had fallen. My mother had always been the strongest person I'd ever known. But now, it was like the drugs had reduced her to nothing more than the average, crazed dope addict in the projects. I got up and wrapped my arms around her. From this close, she smelled so bad it made me emotional. I felt like breaking down. "Mama, I love you, and I'll always be there for you, huh." I knew it was stupid, but I handed her a hundred-dollar-bill. "When it's all said and done, please make sure you get something to eat with this money, before or after you do what you're going to do wit it." I kissed her forehead and stood up. "Come on, Jade, let's get out of here."

***

Back on the subway, I sat with my back to my seat, and my mind all over the place. I still couldn't believe the sight of my mother. Couldn't believe she'd fallen so far off the wagon in such a little time. The drug had taken ahold of her entire life and it made me, in a sense, feel just as weak. I wanted to save her. I wanted to rescue her from the grips of the drug, but I didn't know how. I knew she would never listen to me, and most times when I tried to intervene, all it would lead to was a verbal fight between the two of us. I disliked arguing with my mother, and regardless to how strung out on drugs she was, in my eyes she was still my queen.

Jade reached for my hand and interlocked our fingers again. She leaned over and laid her head on my shoulder. "Are you okay, Bentley? You've been quiet ever since we got on the train."

There were about nine other people on the train. Seven of them had either headphones in their ears or were texting away on their phones. It was flurrying outside and appeared to be getting colder by the minute. I tightened my fingers within hers and turned to her. "I don't like seeing her like that, Jade. Every time I see her in that state, it breaks my heart. I wish I could save my mother. She's still a queen, she's just broken like you and I, but she doesn't have any direction, or anybody to lean on. You know?"

"Yeah, I do. Thankfully, we have each other. Life is so hard, especially when your heart has been broken the way hers has. What do you think you should do?" she asked, rubbing the back of my hand and gazing into my eyes. She smelled so good and looked even better. I'd never liked a female being all up on me the way Jade was. It usually made me feel smothered, but for some reason, her closeness was comforting for me. It was like I needed her to be as such.

I shrugged my shoulders. "I don't know what to do, that's why I'm losing my mind just a lil bit." Every time I thought about her, I felt defeated and got depressed. The only time I felt any sense of relief, or hope is when I brought her a meal and she actually sat down and ate it in front of me. At least then I knew she had some sort of food in her system.

"Well don't worry, Bentley, you'll figure it out. Don't allow it to stress you out the way that it is." She ran her fingers through her hair. "I gotta tell you though. All that talk about the police putting money on my head is freaking me out. You were right when you said we don't know how much more time we have together. I am pretty sure that when they catch me, they are goin' to lock me up for the rest of my life, even though I am innocent. I am so scared, Bentley. I wouldn't know the first thing of how to survive in there. What about my sisters? I wanted to rescue them one day." She lowered her head as if already seeing her fate in her mind. "How could she do this to me? I'm her daughter."

I put my arm around her shoulders and scooted closer to her. "Jade listen to me, I ain't about to let nothing happen to you. I'll kill every one of them pigs if they try and take you away from me. I know you're innocent. She admitted to what she did to him right in front of me, more than once. I ain't about to let you go down for some shit you ain't do, and even if you had, I still ain't going to. It's us against this world right now. You see what my old man trying to do to me. He in the same shit."

She nodded. "Yeah, I heard her. That's so foul. Why would he blame you for an accident? Did you really have somethin' going on with his girl or something, or were you two just wrestling, playing around and stuff?"

The subway pulled into a stop and a few of the passengers got off, then about twenty more boarded. They took seats all around us. One Puerto Rican chick had a five-year-old little boy screaming at the top of his lungs that he wanted to go back with his daddy. She tried to calm him down by pulling him to her chest and hugging him, but this only made him go more berserk. He started screaming so loud, I wanted to get up and whoop his lil ass. I felt it was what he needed.

Jade covered her ears and mugged the little boy and his mother. The little boy started to hit his mother in the face, before taking off running down the subway car with her behind him crying. He wound up crawling under the seat, scooting as far away from her as he could, constantly hollering that he wanted to go back with his daddy.

"Please, Roberto, you will see him next weekend. You have to behave until then. Now please come from under there. You're embarrassing us," she pleaded.

"No, I want my daddy. I love him, and not you. I want him! I want him! Daddy! Daddy!" he hollered.

The Puerto Rican woman, who couldn't have been more than twenty years old, sat in the middle of the aisle and brought her knees to her chest, and wrapped her arms around them. "I don't know what to do. I try so hard," she cried.

I frowned. "What? Shid, I do." I bounced up and made my way to the back of the train where the little boy was. Ducked down and pulled his lil ass out by his arm, threw him over my lap and spanked the shit out of him for thirty full seconds, while he kicked his legs all wild and stuff. When I finished, I put him down, and knelt in front of him. "Now you listen to me, Roberto, that is your mother and you're goin' to respect her. If she have to tell you to do anything else more than once again, I'ma be back, you understand me? Say, yes sir."

"Yes sir." He sniffled, rubbing his backside, with his bottom lip quivering.

I turned to her. "Yo, you whoop his ass. Don't be letting him talk to you like that. That's what's wrong wit kids these days."

She nodded and grabbed her son. "It's just that me and his daddy are going through a custody battle. He sees him every other weekend and gives him everything he wants

146

during their visits, so by the time I get him back, he's like this. I don't know what to do, but I'm so tired of it." She mugged the child angrily.

I wanted to give her a whole spiel, but our stop came up and Jade tapped me on the shoulder. "Come on, Bentley, we're on Broadway, this is our stop."

***

Back at the trap, I couldn't get my mother off my mind, or the things she'd said to us about the police. Me and Jade had to get out of New York, and as soon as possible. I didn't know how much longer we could last in the city without being snatched up. I wasn't ready to go to nobody's jail, especially for a crime I knew I didn't commit, but more important than that, I wasn't ready to be separated from Jade. So, I sat there depressed, trying to think of my next move.

She came out the kitchen with two bowls and a box of cereal. Sat on the living room table, and then went and grabbed the gallon of milk, before coming back to where I was. "Bentley, you looking real sick right now. I don't know what's going on with you, but it is nothing that a bowl of Cap'n Crunch Berries can't solve. Come on, because you're about to eat somethin'." She slid a bowl across the table, along with a spoon.

"Yo, I don't feel like eating nothing right now. My mind all over the place. I feel sick." I searched my jacket for a blunt, and came up empty and got irritated. I needed something to take the edge off.

Jade came around the table, and plopped on the couch beside me. "Care to talk about it?"

"We gotta get out of New York soon. I ain't trying to see nothing bad happen to you, or me. You about ready to go and see what's good wit Sondra?" I was still on the fence about heading over to Jersey. I didn't want to be dependent on another person. I really didn't like the fact that I would be in a place where I didn't really know what was going on. But New York could no longer be an option, our time was running out. We had to relocate, and New Jersey was the only place I could think of on such short notice.

"I been texting her, but she ain't hit me back yet. As soon as she do, we're out of here. I guess that stuff your mother said is starting to mess with you too, huh?" She stroked my hand, then laid her head on my shoulder. I liked when she did that, for some reason.

"Yeah, you know how thirsty mafuckas in Brooklyn are. Twelve talking about money. It's only a matter of time before the whole city is out looking for us to make a profit. We gotta bounce soon. I ain't ready for us to be split apart, are you?"

She shook her head. "We're just getting to know each other. That wouldn't be cool at all. So, what do you propose? Should we just head out there, and try our luck?"

"Hell naw. She gon be hitting you back in a minute, right?"

"Yeah, she should. She usually gets right back to me. I don't know what's going on."

"Well, we'll just kick back until then, and go from there. I still got a little over ten bands tucked away so we're good money-wise, for now. Once she hit you up, we'll roll out that way. Sound like a plan?"

She looked up at me and smiled. "It does." She picked her head up. "Bentley, you never did answer my question either and I need you to."

"What question was that, Jade?" I rubbed along her shoulder blades, then across her back very lightly. I didn't know if it hurt or not, every time she was barely touched there.

She turned around to look at me. "The question about your dad's girl. You guys were just cool, right? Like, there wasn't any funny business or anything like that was there?"

I scrunched my face. "What?"

"No, the reason I'm asking is because your mother was making it seem like ol' girl was crazy over you or something. Then, if you had to block her all over social media, that just sounds like more than a son and mother-in-law type of relationship. You know what I mean?"

I felt my heart pounding in my chest. I didn't know which lane to travel with Jade. If she found out I was fucking my father's wife, there was no way she could ever trust me again. She could also potentially think I was guilty of what I was being accused of doing. That could both scare and turn her off from me. Two things I couldn't risk. I had a thing for her, and I wanted her to be a part of my life. Our stories were too similar. My attraction to her was way too strong for me to release. So, while it broke my soul to lie to her for the first time, I just didn't see any other way. "Yeah, I know what you mean."

"So, it wasn't nothin' like that? Y'all were strictly on the up and up?"

I nodded. "Of course, ma. That's my pops' wife, what type of nigga would I be?" I felt sick as soon as the words left my tongue. There was the first lie. I prayed it didn't taint whatever we were on our way to building.

"Aw, I ain't think no crap like that, but I just had to ask. Wanted to know what I was walking into. I'm from a crazy family too, so I really can't judge you. I can accept whatever I have to, just as long as I know what's good up front." She smiled, and turned away. "Life is so hard. Thank God I found a good person like you though, Bentley. Both of us are being accused for things we didn't do. Both of us are fighting against this cold, cold world to cleanse our tarnished names. We're all we have. "That's crazy, ain't it?"

I wanted to tell her the truth right then, but no matter how much I tried to fix my brain to tell her the truth, it wouldn't let me. I was too afraid of how it would make her look at me. So, I held my tongue and essentially, the truth from her. "Everything happens for a reason, Jade. Everything."

Chapter 13

Jade

Thanksgiving 2018

I was running around like a chicken with my head cut off. I don't know why I thought I would be able to prepare an entire Thanksgiving meal on my own for the first time. I'd bitten off more than I could chew, and I was too embarrassed to admit that to Bentley.

I bent over and opened the oven door. Pulled out the turkey and stuck the digital thermometer inside of it. Just as Bentley slipped into the kitchen, and came from behind me, pulling me into his arms from behind. Laying a light kiss on my cheek. "Jade, you got it smelling real good in here, ma. Do you need any help?"

I smiled. "Thank you, Bentley." Lord knows I wanted to tell him yes. I had so many things to do. I was feeling overwhelmed, but my pride got in the way. "Nall, I'm good. I'm making it happen. You just gon back in there and watch the game. Let me do my thing in here. I gotta put my toe in everything I whip up, you feel me?" I wish I had as much confidence as I was fronting to have. I was so worried about how everything was going to turn out, my heart wouldn't stop beating like crazy.

He pressed his lips against my cheek again. "Yo, you sure, ma? It seem like you got plenty left to do, and I don't like leaving you out on the limb like this. Besides, the sooner you get done in here, the sooner I can be in there boo-ed up like Ella Mai."

I laughed at his word play. "Well, if you let me go, I can do my thing. I'm about two hours out from having everything done. I gotta make sure that this is the best Thanksgiving you've ever had. So scoot. I'll be in there as soon as I'm done."

He held me more firm. "Aiight, I'ma hold you to that. I appreciate the slaving too, queen, word up, you ain't have to do none of this. It means a lot."

"Bentley, as long as you appreciate it then it's all worth it. It's the least I can do to show you my gratitude. I'm thankful for you. I mean that with all of my heart."

He nuzzled his face into the crook of my neck and kissed it with his hot lips. "Yeah, well I'm tryna show my appreciation later. I want this to be the best Thanksgiving you've ever had as well." He bit my neck and growled.

That sent tingles all over my body. The heat from the oven traveled up the Prada skirt I was wearing, further igniting me. "See you in a minute, ma." He kissed the side of my neck, and walked into the living room after taking one of the pineapple slices from the table and tossing it into his mouth. He had on a black beater and his back muscles were prominent. He looked and smelled like a god. I had to shake my head to get back on track.

We never got the chance to head out to New Jersey, because before we were able to, Sondra had found out that she was pregnant, and went and moved in with the father of her unborn child. After that transition, she'd been very stand offish. Barely on social media, she rarely ever answered my texts or Facebook messages. I didn't know what her problem was. I was just thankful that Bentley and I had not rolled all the way out to New Jersey, only to be turned back around. I am sure that would have been a strain on the friendship we were building, amongst other things.

Life of Sin

There was a knock on the door. "Bentley, you gon get that?" I hollered, and pushed the turkey back into the oven. It was at ninety-seven degrees in its center. I estimated I had at least another forty minutes of cooking to do before it was ready to be carved up. I side-stepped to the sink and started to shuck my peas. The collard greens were already on the stove bubbling, I added a touch of vinegar, and a pinch of Lawry's seasoned salt, stored them, and went right back to shucking my peas. It brought me back to a time when me and my mother would be in the kitchen, preparing a Thanksgiving for the family while the twins played with their toys, and we both prayed my father came home in a decent mood. My mother had never actually sat me down and taught me how to cook. I literally learned just by watching her. I felt emotional at the flashbacks. My family had not been perfect, but they were all I had.

Bentley walked into the kitchen with his arm around some Puerto-Rican-looking female's neck. I don't know why, but I got instantly jealous. I wanted to know who she was and their relation. I couldn't think of any man outside of him that I would have allowed to place their arm around my neck, especially not at this juncture of our relationship.

"Yo Jade, this is Milan, Santana's lil piece. Milan, this is my…" He paused and looked over at me.

I dried my hand in a towel, and shook Milan's hand, eyeing Bentley. "My name is Jade, and I am Bentley's friend. It's nice to meet you." *So, this is the famous Milan,* I thought, looking her up and down. She was very pretty, with her short curly hair and perfectly applied make-up and tight Gucci dress that molded to her curvy frame. She looked like she was a model by day and stripped by night.

Her hands were soft and perfumed. "It's very nice to meet you, Jade. I see why Bentley has been cooped up in the house the last few months. Santana's words, not mine."

I scoffed, and took that as a compliment. "Yeah, well I don't control Bentley, if he's been in the house for whatever reason, I can assure you it isn't just because of me. Excuse me." I shot him a glance and went back to getting my peas ready. I didn't like the fact that he'd paused when it came to introducing me. It affected my self-esteem. I wondered if he was embarrassed by me or something. Or, maybe he didn't want her to know he had a thing for me. She was pretty, and he was in fact a dope boy that was used to having real bad females. Maybe his honest opinion of me was that I wasn't bad enough. That angered me even more. Suddenly, I didn't even want to finish the meal.

Milan came up beside me. "Hey would you mind if I gave you a hand? I don't really like football, and I don't want to be the only girl in the living room either. Besides, I love to cook. I promise not to get into your way."

I wanted to tell her to get her ass out of the kitchen. I didn't feel like catching a headache from her stanky ass perfume, and I didn't want her crowding my space. I had always been a solitary female. Wasn't good at making friends with girls. They were too catty for me. Too competitive, and too nosey. On top of all that, I didn't have the strongest self-esteem. I was always comparing myself to them. Milan was gorgeous and had an air about herself that made me feel insecure and uncomfortable.

Bentley came over to me and slid his arm around my shoulder. "Gon 'head and let her, Jade, or else she ain't gon do nothin' but be in the way. Besides, looking around, I see you can use the help." He laughed.

I mugged his ass, and didn't find his joke funny one bit. What, he must've thought that just because she was all dolled up, she was going to save the day. Now I really wanted to throw her ass out of there.

"Honestly, Bentley, it looks like she's done one hell of a job. Everything smells good, and looks good. I was hoping to do some of the remaining grunt work, that's all," Milan added.

Yeah bitch, that's right, be smooth, I thought. I gathered she could tell I wasn't feeling her presence in the kitchen at all. "Yeah, it's cool, I can use the help. Thank you, Milan. Here, you can come help me get these peas ready before I pull the turkey out in a little while."

She smiled, and screeched deep within her throat. "That sounds amazing."

Bentley went into the refrigerator, and grabbed out two Budweisers. "Y'all make this shit happen in here while I go holler at my mans. Play nice too in here. I already know how shit get when two dimes try and do one job. Make sure y'all keep them claws put up," he joked.

I mugged his ass and was seconds away from checking him in front of her and Santana. I didn't like how he was coming at me as if I was some kind of housewife, waiting on him hand and foot. And, I didn't like being coupled in with another female that I didn't know. I was disturbed and vexed at the same time.

Milan looked over her shoulder at him. "Well, at least you called me a dime, that's all that matter to me. We gon get it right in here, ain't we, Jade?"

I sucked my teeth, "Bentley, go watch the game. The food a' be done when it's done," I snapped and turned away from him.

He left the kitchen laughing and I didn't see shit funny. I wanted to elbow her ass too. She kept her eyes glued on him all the way until he left the kitchen, then shook her head. "Damn, he so fine. Are y'all together?" she asked, going back to work in an almost dream-like state. There was this weird look on her face that made me jealous.

"Why do you ask me that? That's a personal question. We just met not more than five minutes ago."

"Oh, I didn't mean no disrespect. I was just wondering, because I know he's still talking to Keri off and on, but supposedly they aren't serious. Santana said he was fucking his father's woman too. Bentley is a handful, but he's so fine. If y'all ain't together, you better find a way to lock him down. I definitely wouldn't mind doing so." She ran her tongue over her glossed lips, and sucked on her bottom one. "He can fuck too, but I'm sure you already know that."

I slammed my hand on the rim of the sink. "Damn, bitch, ain't you fucking wit Santana?"

She shrugged her shoulders. "We cool, but he ain't got no papers on me. He know I got a thing for Bentley. He let me suck his dick and everything, but that ain't enough. I watched as he did Keri. I gotta get me a piece of him, I mean, if y'all ain't fucking around of course." She placed a handful of peas into the strainer I had on the right side of the sink.

"Milan, I get the impression that even if you knew me and Bentley were together, you'd still try and fuck him. It just seems like it's in your nature to do so. So, what are your true intentions for asking to help me cook? You wanted to spill some tea on Bentley, huh? You wanted to drop a few dirty jewels to see if you could loosen up what you think me and him got going, because y'all ain't seen him in the streets in a while? Huh, bitch, is that it? You wanna fuck him that bad?"

Milan laughed. "Girl please, if I wanted Bentley, I would've had him already. Have you taken a good look at me, I mean really looked?" She took a step back and waved her hand over herself to emphasize her point. "I'm what you would call a bad bitch. Not mediocre."

I looked her up and down and pursed my lips, bringing them to the right side of my face before smacking them loudly. "Bitch, you ain't all that. It would take me five minutes to beat that pretty off you. And just by listening to your conversation, I can tell that that's all you are is pretty, so once that's gone, you gon be in a world of trouble." I leaned into her face. "I don't know what you think this is, but I'ma let you know right now, you fucking wit the wrong one. If you try and come onto him in any way while I'm around, I'ma be forced to bring this Red Hook shit out of me, and trust me, you don't want those problems. You feel me?" I leered into her eyes, unblinking.

She swallowed. "Yeah, I feel you. Like I said, I didn't mean no disrespect." Her voice was shaky. She sounded terrified, as she should have been. I was seconds off her ass.

***

"Aw, shit. My word, I can't eat another bite. Jade, you did ya thing wit this meal, ma, word up," Santana complimented me, scooting his chair back from the table. He pulled up his shirt and rubbed his stomach in a circular motion.

Milan moved his hand out of the way and began to rub it for him. "Yeah, girl, I'm stuffed. You should let me pay you back with a spa day. I'll foot the entire bill. We can get beauty treatments and all of that shit." She groaned and rubbed her own stomach. "What do you say?"

Bentley cut in. "Yo, if she wanna have a spa day, I'll make that happen. She can have a spa week if she want it. She good." He scooted away from the table as well and struggled to breathe. "Yo, the Bears killing the Lions, kid. Detroit sucks," he related and rubbed his stomach.

I watched him for a short time, then turned to Milan. "Thank you for the offer. That was pretty generous of you. Let me think it over."

Bentley shot me a glance. "Stop playing wit me, Jade. You know I got you. I don't need no help holding you down."

"Bentley, watch that game. She was talking to me and not you. And I said what I said." I rolled my eyes at him and stood up, taking my used plate off the table and walking into the kitchen with it.

He showed up seconds later and slid beside me just as I was dumping the food scraps into the trash. "Yo, what's your problem, Jade? Why you acting all funny and shit?" His breath smelled like cranberry sauce and dressing.

"I ain't got no problem, I just don't like you answering for me like I'm your property or something. Don't nobody own me, if I wanted to accept her gift of appreciation then I would, and you couldn't stop me from doing that because you don't own me and I'm not one of your hoez. I'm my own woman. You need to get that through your head, seriously." I bumped him out of my way and placed my plate in the sink, rinsing, and washing it out. I was becoming irritated, and I didn't want to do what we were getting ready to do in front of Santana and Milan. But, I knew Bentley wasn't about to take what I was saying lying down. I'd gotten to know his character quite a bit over the past few months we had been in close quarters with one another.

He came up behind me. "Jade, why you flexing on me right now? What that bitch say to you?" he asked with his face balled up. He looked angry. His eyes were low and turning red.

"Nothing I shouldn't have already known." I soaped up the dish and rinsed it out, before setting it in the dish drain to dry.

He stormed out of the kitchen and into the living room. "Bitch, stand up. What the fuck you tell my queen?" He grabbed her by the arm and flung her toward the kitchen. She stumbled into it and crashed into the table.

"Damn, Bentley, I ain't tell her shit. Why you bugging, B?"

She rubbed her elbow that had slammed into the table, looked over at me then back to him. "What she tell you I said?"

"Yo, Santana, I'm about to whoop yo bitch's ass if she don't tell me what's good. I know she been in here clucking at my Earth. Jade ain't acted this funny toward me in a long time."

Santana stood up. "That ain't got nothing to do wit me. If you whoop her ass, she gotta accept that. Bitches need to keep they mouth closed anyway or get somethin stuck in it. Just hurry up and do what you gon do, 'cause me and this bitch got some bidness to handle before the night out."

Milan backed away from Bentley. "Look, Bentley, why don't I tell you what I said and we'll go from there? She probably lying anyway. Bitches always hating on me." She looked over at me with hate in her eyes.

Just as I was about to save her from getting her ass whooped she had to say something like that. "Bitch, you gotta be out of your mind. Ain't nobody hating on you. You run your mouth way too much. Talking 'bout how Santana watched you suck his dick, and you watched him fuck Keri. Oh, and apparently, you were fucking your father's woman, according to her." I crossed my arms, feeling petty as hell but not caring because her comments had pissed me off to begin with.

Bentley snapped his neck to look at her and the next thing I knew, he'd lost it.

Chapter 14

Bentley

I grabbed Milan by her neck and lifted her in the air before I could stop myself from doing it. I couldn't fathom what would make her tell Jade everything she had. That had me pissed. I held her up against the wall with one hand, while she beat at my hand so I could drop her, but I wasn't going. "You stupid bitch! What's your problem? What the fuck is wrong wit you?"

She gagged. Her eyes rolled into the back of her head.

Jade ran over. "Bentley. Bentley. Let her down. Let her down. Please don't kill this girl!" she screamed.

Santana stood at a safe distance. He knew my temper. Knew that when I blew my lid, it was best to give me my space. "Yo, she out of order, Dunn. If kid gon choke her out, then when he done, I'ma bury this bitch. Word is bond."

"Please, Bentley. Please don't do this," Jade begged, holding my arm.

I was so mad that I squeezed Milan's neck harder. I had every intention on choking her ass out, until I looked into Jade's eyes and saw how terrified she was. She had the same look in her eyes the night the men had tried to rape her. I never took the time out to think of how much damage this could have been doing to her. This, alongside of everything Milan had told her would surely work against me. The last thing I wanted to do was to go backwards with our relationship, but I had so much damage control to do that I felt defeated and a bit dismayed. I dropped Milan to the floor.

She fell on her ass, her knees to her chest, holding her neck. "I'm sorry, Bentley." Coughed and sounded like she was still choking. "I ain't mean to tell her all that."

"Bitch, get the fuck out of my crib! You better be lucky she had me fall back off yo ass. Get the fuck out, now!"

She jumped to her feet, ran into the living room and grabbed her purse, before scampering to the door and unlocking it. "Santana, are you coming?"

He waved her off. "Bitch, I'll meet you at the truck. Get yo punk ass out like blood said. Hurry up."

She nodded and left the apartment, closing the door behind her.

"Yo, thank y'all for the meal, man. On the real, this has been one of the best Thanksgivings on record for me. That was, until that bitch got to yapping. Bentley, I'ma fuck wit you in a minute. I should have a nice piece of change lined up for us tomorrow, or the next day."

I mugged him. "Nigga, next time you wanna do some pillow talking wit that bitch, talk about somebody else. I know I'm constantly on her mental, but y'all talk about somebody else, word up."

He took a step forward. "What you tryna say, nigga?"

"Nigga, you know what I'm saying. I ain't speaking in Morse code. Keep my name out y'all bedroom. Pillow talk about another nigga. Point-blank." I balled my fists. My heart was beating so fast, I was nearly out of breath. I was getting madder and madder by the second. I didn't know what was wrong with me, but I was ready to wile out.

Santana clenched his jaw, and sucked his teeth. "Yo, I don't know what you talking about, or why you huffin' and puffin' at the god, but I'ma let you have this one and fuck wit you tomorrow. Y'all have a nice evening and thank you for the dinner." He took one more glance at me, before he stepped out the house and closed the door behind him, shaking his head.

As soon as the door closed, Jade snapped. "Bentley, I swear to God, you remind me of my fucking father! Why would you do that girl like that?"

"Man, she in there telling you all of this bullshit for no reason! What's the point for all that? Huh?"

"So that gives you a reason to out your hands in her, huh? So, whenever me and you have a disagreement, you gone choke me out too? Have me all up against the wall with my legs swinging below me? Bentley, I swear to God, I'm not gon ever let you do me like you did her. I've been through that enough with my own father. You're supposed to be different!"

"Jade, I would never do you like that. I care about you way too much. That bitch was just bogus. She ain't have no right salting me like that, and you know it." I walked toward her and she stepped backward.

"Bentley, tell me she wasn't telling the truth about you and your father's woman? Tell me she was lying right now or we're going to have a serious problem. I mean that."

Lying came across my mind once again. It would have been so easy. Just one more lie and then everything would go back to the way it had been before Santana and Milan had shown up. I felt so stupid for inviting them over now. I should've spent the entire holiday with Jade. That's what my first mind had told me. I was seriously regretting not going with it. "Jade, I don't want to lie to you again. The shit wit me and my pops' bitch is real complicated. You see..."

She waved me off. "You know what? I ain't got time for this shit. You just said you lied to begin with. I'd be a damn fool to sit here and hear you out, when I know damn well you ain't about to do nothing but lie through your fucking teeth. Ugh! I thought I could trust you." She turned her back and headed to the bedroom. Opened the closet and grabbed a duffle bag from the floor, before taking her clothes off the hangers and stuffing them inside the bag. "All I asked was for you to tell me the truth. I asked you that more than once. You couldn't even do that."

I slowly walked into the room feeling like shit. Not only had I lied to her, but I'd snatched up a female in her face and reminded her of her father in the process. I was no different than him in that moment. I didn't know what I could possibly say to her. Everything seemed wrong. "Jade, please hear me out. I ain't mean to lie to you, ma. Shit just real complicated. I didn't know how to explain to you what went down between me and her. You wouldn't have understood."

She turned around and pointed in my face. "You didn't give me a chance to understand. You deprived me of that right. You made the choice for me and treated me just like one of them nobody females in the street. I thought we had more of a connection than that. That you respected me more than that. But it turns out, all you see is what you can and can't control, typical." She looked me up and down and scoffed, before packing her bag again.

"Jade, on everything I need you, ma. I ain't fuckin' around no more. I'm tryna start fresh with you. I apologize for not giving you that chance to make a decision for yourself, but I feared the decision you would make. I ain't never had a female that was just like me before. I ain't never felt the way I do about you, with no other woman. Yo, I'm sorry, baby, please believe me. I wanted to explain myself and give you the truth, but I was terrified of losing you. You been through so much. It's so hard for you to trust me. Me telling you what went on with her wouldn't have been anything other than a major setback. Now, tell me I'm wrong."

She turned around. "You're wrong. Bentley, what you did before you and I met is your past. Who am I to judge you for your past, when we both come from the depths of hell? Lies will always shatter me more than the truth. I don't understand how men don't get that? A woman will always be more willing to accept you for your upfront truths, then for your 'down the road' discovered lies. You have to give me the chance to accept you for you. We have been lied to enough. Between you and I, our truths and our devotion to each other is all that we have. I need to know you are always one hunnit wit me. If I can't, what's the point?" She knelt down and stuffed more designer clothes into the bag.

I dropped yo my knees beside her. "I never felt nothing for her. The only reason I smashed her like a jump-off on so many occasions, is because it was my way of getting back at my father for leaving my mother. To clap back at him for the pain he put her through. For driving her to crack. For making her try and kill me, because I was a mere image of him. Every time I slept with her, it was out of spite and never love. I was betraying him like he'd done my mother. Because of him, my mother had almost taken my life. I will never forgive him for that. I will never forgive him for driving her to crack. Please don't go, Jade. I care about you. I need you in my life. Don't you see how fucked up I am? How lost? You can't leave me like this." I don't know how it started, but my eyes began to water, before they spilled over and ran down my cheeks. "I need you, Jade. Damn, I fucked up, baby. Please don't go."

She looked over her shoulder at me, then dropped her head. "Bentley, what are you doing? I can't see you like that."

"Like what, vulnerable? I ain't never broke down in front of nobody. Always had to be tough to get by but you know what, Jade, I ain't faking the funk no more. I need you and I'ma fight for you. I'll never lie to you again. I'll always keep it one hunnit wit you. Just please don't go, I'll do anything." I took ahold of her arm and pulled her into my embrace. Heard her crying and that broke me down even further.

"I'm not ready to go through this, Bentley. My heart is not ready. It's too premature. I have to get out of here. You're affecting me in such a way." Her body began to shake.

"Jade please. You can't leave me. I need you. You're the only one in this world I truly need. Before you nothing made sense for me. This world was filled with so much pain. I felt so alone. But then, it's like you were thrust into my life from out of nowhere, and ever since you got here, it's like I am no longer alone. There is finally somebody that can stand beside me and understand my pain. Somebody whom I can relate to on so many levels. I need you, Jade."

She hugged me and her face went into the crook of my neck. Her hand cuffed the back of my head. Her nails lightly scratched me in an endearing fashion. She felt so soft. Smelled so good. "I need you too, Bentley. I need you just as much as you need me, but you have to change. You have to. You can't lie to me whenever you think it is suitable. I need to know I can trust you. I need to know you are the one person in this world I can trust more than anybody else. All we have is our word, Bentley. Without it, and coming from the places of pain we hail from, we are nothin'. Do you understand that?"

"I do, Jade. I swear I do, and I'll never lie to you again." I took her face within the palms of my hands, wiped away her tears, and laid my forehead against hers. "I'm sorry, baby." My lips searched and found her soft pillow-like ones. I kissed them tenderly at first, then sucked on them and pulled her into me. She moaned into my mouth. I pulled back and looked into her dime face, before kissing her with more passion, sucking and licking all over her lips.

"Mmmm, Bentley. No more lies. No more. You promise?" She opened her mouth, then clamped down on my lips with her own. Her breathing grew labored. The arms around my neck tightened, pulling me into her.

"I promise, baby." I guided her back and straddled her body. Leaned down and kissed all over her hot neck. Running my tongue along its length. Tracing it with my teeth, before sucking on her.

"Un, Bentley. Your lips feel so good to me. But, I don't know if I'm ready for this."

My tongue traced a line up her neck, to her earlobe. Once there, I sucked it into my mouth, then added my tongue into her canal. Breathed into it. "We can go slow, Jade. I just wanna be with you. I need to feel you, please." My lips traveled down her neck, and sucked the groove in between her full breasts. The scent of her perfume was heavy here as if it had been the site she'd applied it the most. My tongue flickered from side to side.

"No." She pushed me away, and sat up. Got to her feet and sat on the bed. Lowered her head. "Why do you want me so bad, Bentley? Why am I so different, and when will my scars become a factor? If females like Milan are going to be chasing you the entire time you and I are struggling to be together, sooner or later you're going to give in. I could never stand next to a woman as beautiful as her. I'm just me."

I sat on the bed beside her, and kissed her cheek. "Lay down, Jade. Please. I just need for you to trust me."

She blinked and jerked her head backward. "What?"

"Come on, ma, just trust me." I gave her my most award-winning smile.

She raised her right eyebrow, and exhaled. "Aiight. I'ma trust you, Bentley, but boy, you just don't know where I'm at mentally." She lay on her back and scooted up to the pillows.

"Nall, ma, lay on yo stomach and take that blouse off."

"What?"

"Baby, please." I closed the door and lit an incense. Threw on a cut by R. Kelly called, "Heart of a Woman", from the *Chocolate Factory* album. It was a throwback, but the words were on point.

Jade slid the blouse over her arms and off. Laid it on the bed beside her, took one glance over her shoulder at me, then laid on her arms. "Be careful, Bentley."

I turned on the two lamps in the room and climbed into the bed with a bottle of edible coconut oil. I straddled her waist. "Baby, I need for you to know that you are the most beautiful woman in all the world to me." I lowered my head and kissed her soft shoulder.

Chapter 15

Jade

At the first touch of his lips, my body gave in to multiple tingles. They traveled up and down my spine. Gave me goose bumps. I wanted to tell him to stop right away. To get off me because I wasn't ready. I didn't know when I would be, but this was too premature.

He kissed the bottom of my neck, then trailed his tongue down to the top portion of the middle of my back, then stopped at the first scar. "Jade, I'll do anything for you. I'm already crazy over you, ma. Ever since you came into my life, I've felt like a better man, a stronger man. You are my rib." He was silent, then I felt kisses all over my back. All over the scars my mother had created out of hatred for me. His thick lips traveled up and down my wounds of pain. "I love this body, Jade. You are perfect to me, ma. Perfect in every single way. I can't be without you, baby. I saw what that felt like, and I was so lost. Lost and on my way to never being found again." More kissing, his lips felt hot and moist. The sounds were enough to drive me crazy. I lay there confused, yet in ecstasy. I wished I could read his mind to know for a fact that everything he said out of his mouth was the actual truth. I'd been broken for so long that it was hard to believe him. Hard to believe any man could feel for me the way that he said he was feeling. What was so special about me? I needed to know, as I felt his tongue lick all over my back, before kissing the length of it again.

"Bentley, what's so special about me? What is it about me that you can't find in another female that's way more pretty? Much more deserving? Please tell me, I need to know."

He kissed along my spine, causing me to arch my back. "Jade, you're not like any other female I've ever come across, because I be knowing deep down in my heart you were created for me. When I'm with you, I don't see anybody else. All I see is us and all that matters is you. You are my portion, only you, Jade." He sat up and rubbed all over my back. "I wish I could have been there. I wish I could have been there to protect you from this abuse, Jade. You're so precious." I heard the top to the oil pop open and then he squirted what I imagine was a hefty portion into the palms of his hands, because the next thing I knew, he was massaging it into my back. "These scars are your jewels, Jade. They are one of the most precious things that set you aside from everybody else. They are what make you unique. I love them." He lowered his head again and kissed all over me, taking his time to massage certain areas, before his lips were worshipping my imperfections again.

I lay with my face on my arms, stuck in limbo. A part of me wanted to succumb to the administering, the worshipping, and the tender affection he took time out to relay unto me. I needed his healing so, so much. I needed him to keep fighting for me, to keep saying the words because they made me feel special. They made me feel rare. How could any man see all the harmful work my mother had done to my back, see it in all of its dark glory, and still want to desire, cater to, and be with me? I didn't get it. I couldn't see it, but I also could not see the hidden agenda underneath it all, even though the insecurities within my soul were trying so desperately to create quite a few for me. "Bentley,...."

He licked along my spine, all the way down to the hemline of my lacy boy short underwear. Peeled it back, then ran his tongue where the band had once been, before reaching underneath my body and undoing my skirt. I stopped his hands. "Baby, chill, I know where you are mentally, but you also gotta know where I am as well. I got you, just trust me. Please."

I started to shake, but laid back down, doing something I had not done in a very long time. I trusted him, even though I was scared out of my mind at what his next moves would be. I prepared myself and lay back down.

Bentley took ahold of my skirt, and pulled it down my thighs and off my ankles. Dropped it to the floor and next came my black stockings. They followed the same path until I was laying there in anticipation of what was next to come. "All I see is you, Jade. My vision of you will never change, because you are my reflection. We are the same person. You are my rib. I ain't never felt this way about nobody." He parted my legs, his lips wound up on my right shoulder, then he was sucking on my neck, slightly nipping with his teeth. "I got you, Jade. I'ma hold you down, ma. Me. All by myself. I won't fail you." He kissed down my back, along my spine, then back down to my lower back. His big hands slid over my backside, rubbed me there, then kneaded the cheeks in his hands. "Damn, Jade, you so fuckin' fine."

I started to shake. I was afraid. His hands felt so good, but so wrong at the same time. I wanted to get up and roll with the punches at the same time. So far, the punches had pushed me out of my comfort zone, and into space I had never been in before. My adrenalin pumped as I wondered where the journey would lead me. How far would I allow him to go? And what risks would he take, knowing how I felt before he started to do what he was?

I felt his hot breath on the back of my thighs. He kissed the left one, sucked it, then trailed his tongue to the right, and did the same with that one. "You're so beautifully made, Jade. Ain't nobody like you." His tongue traveled up my inner thighs, until they got to the crotch band of my under-wear. Once there, he applied more kisses over the material.

On their own accord, my thighs tried to close, but he held them open, and nudged them further apart. "Bentley, I just wanna," were the only words that came out of my mouth, before he licked up and down the crotch, pushing the lace into my valley. His thumb searched for my groove's nipple. It took him no time to find it. After locating it, he pressed in it, then applied more kisses all over my box. I was getting hot and bothered, breathing heavy and feening for him to go on, and to stop at the same time.

He pulled the material to the side, exposing my most secret treasure to his eyes. Groaned deep within his throat. I felt embarrassed. I knew that I was beyond wet. I could feel my essence pouring out of me. "I just wanna treasure you, Jade. Is that so wrong? I just wanna make you happy, and protect you for the rest of my life." I looked over my shoulder in time to see his head disappear behind me. The next thing I felt were my lips being sucked into his mouth, and his tongue separating the folds at the same time, diving into me.

I arched my back and glanced over my shoulder, looking for him. "Bentley. Baby, you're…"

He popped my lips out, and sucked them in again. Opened me up, and licked along each side of my kitty, while his big hands massaged my backside. "Your taste, Jade. Damn, baby, your taste." He ran circles around my clitoris, trapped the bud, tugging on it, then flicking it over and over with his tongue, before inhaling it, slurping loudly.

I grabbed handfuls of the sheets and closed my eyes tight. Bit into my bottom lip to keep from emitting a moan that would embarrass me. I'd never felt the feelings he was rendering unto me. No one had ever done what he was. I'd heard about my friends talking about the act, but as a reality, it was foreign to me. And it felt so good. I felt so trapped and lost.

He opened me wide, and spent ten minutes between my crease, licking and twirling, sucking and darting, until I couldn't take it anymore. All the stress and all of my past pain came rushing from all over my body. I squeezed my eyelids together and started to shake as if I was having a seizure. "Bentley! Bentley! Oh my God, baby!" I whimpered as my orgasm came rushing over me like a tidal wave, leaving me trembling for sixty straight seconds.

He continued to lick and suck. His word were muffled in between my legs. "It's only you, Jade. You're my world now, ma. Just you. I'll never fail you, boo, never." More slurping, sending me into another violent orgasm.

After this one, I flipped over and brought my knees to my chest. "Wait, Bentley. Please, I gotta catch my breath." My heart was thumping in my chest.

He crawled up the bed and took me into his arms. "We ain't gotta go no further than that, Jade. I just needed to taste you. I needed to submit to you in some way. I swear, I'm becoming nuts over you." He laid my head in his chest, and rubbed my shoulder. "Did I go too far?"

There were tingles still shooting all over my body. My sex was fully awakened. Quivering. My essence oozed out of me, and into the crotch of my panties. "I don't know. But, I'll be okay." I looked up at him and saw he was looking down at me with a sense of worry in his eyes. I smiled and squeezed my thighs together to stop the insatiable feeling in between them. "Thank you, Bentley. Thank you for not going any further than that and for saying all the things you did. Just please never lie to me again, and mean what you said. Show me with your actions and if you will, I promise to live up to the vision of me that you see. Can you do that?"

He smiled, his handsome face beaming. "For you, Jade, I'll do anything because you're worth it." He hugged me tighter. "You're my rib, I hope you know that." Kissed the side of my forehead and kept his lips planted against my skin.

"Oh yeah, what makes you say that?" I wanted to know.

"Because my uncle, who is the pastor of a church, always told me that when a man runs across the woman that God created for him, his rib, he's going to know it because this woman will make him feel like no other. She will turn his world upside down, and nothing or no one will ever be able to compare to her. That's how I feel about you, Jade. You have turned my world upside down. Nobody compares to you. All I see is you, and I ain't checking for nobody else. I just wanna make you happy, is that so wrong?" he asked, and stroking my hair, then his hand wondered down to my naked back.

"I just pray that your feelings don't change. You are taking me away, Bentley. Please, I hope you know what you're doing, because I sure don't. Come on, I need you to hold me for a little while." I scooted down on the bed, and he spooned behind me, snuggling up close. His cologne sent me on a silent journey. My lady parts were screaming out for him.

"Yo Jade, you tryna steal my G-card, ma. Word is bond, I ain't never felt so sappy in my life. I need to whoop a nigga a' something." He laughed and kissed the back of neck.

"You're good, Bentley. I know it ain't sweet. You make me feel so good. I'm thankful for you."

"I'm thankful for you, baby. Now zone out wit me, I just want to hold you."

"Bentley, you know I feel your mans down low throbbing against me, right? You sure holding me is all you wanna do?" I asked, already knowing the truth, but I just wanted to see what he was going to say.

"Yo, good night, queen. I said I ain't gon lie to you no more, so fall back and let me enjoy what I am getting from yo bad ass."

I snickered. "Good night."

***

For the rest of the night, he held me protectively in his big arms. I couldn't stop smiling. Every time my eyes opened and I felt him holding me the way he was, I just could not feel more secure, or thankful. I prayed the current feelings he held for me never left. I needed him just as much as he needed me.

Chapter 16

Bentley

The sounds of a car slamming on its brakes jarred me awake. I sat straight up in bed, on high alert. Jade lay at my side lightly snoring. She sucked her thumb in her sleep and looked so adorable. I leaned forward and kissed her on the forehead. Then, there was an insistent banging on the front door that made me hop out the bed, rush to the dresser and pull my Glock .40 out of it before stepping into the hallway, and closing the bedroom door behind me. Ten steps away from the door and the knocking ensued again, more vigorously than before. I looked through the peephole and saw Santana standing in front of the door, with blood all over his face. One of his eyes was closed. There was black all around it. He looked as if he was seconds away from panicking, or freaking out. His hand reached to knock again.

"Yo, who is it?" I cocked the Glock, and placed my fingers on the locks to the door.

"It's me, Bentley, open up. I just got twisted, B." He looked both ways and wiped blood from his lip.

Jade appeared in the hallway, wiping the sleep out of her eyes. "Bentley, what's going on? I thought you were going to hold me all night?"

"It's morning, Jade, it's like five o'clock. Go back to bed. I'll be there in a minute." I waved her off.

"But, why do you have that out?" She pointed at the gun, and turned her head sideways.

"Jade, just go in there. It's Santana at the door. I think he hurt."

She took three steps backward and nodded. "Okay, but hurry up, Bentley." She disappeared into the room, and left the door ajar. I sighed and pulled open the door for Santana. He walked in past me, shaking his head. "Damn, nigga, you gon leave a mafucka in the hallway all morning? What if somebody was chasing me?" he asked, looking over his shoulder at me.

"Nigga, never mind that. What the fuck happened to you?" I tucked my pistol in the small of my back and closed the door, locking it.

He wiped his mouth again. "That bitch, Milan, she set me up. I just got twisted for two hundred and fifty bands in the Bronx. I need you to roll over there and get my money back with me. I know where they took it and one of my homes already in place. I just need to make sure I got a hitta on beside me that I trust. And I don't trust nobody like I trust you, god, word is bond."

I frowned and looked him over. "How you know she had something to do wit it, first of all? Second of all, how do you know them niggas about to be over at this trap, if they just hit yo ass up for all that cake?" It was too early in the morning to be fucking around with Santana. I was irritated and sexually frustrated because of the night I'd had with Jade. I loved the binding aspect of it, but physically, I was going through it. It had been a few months since I'd gotten some, and whenever my physical wasn't intact, I was short with damn near everybody.

"My lil nigga that's on the inside told me what it was. He sixteen and hustle for one of the niggas that hit me up. He's also Milan's cousin's baby daddy. Long story, but his intel is one hunnit. We gotta get over there while the getting is good. That's two hundred bands, Dunn, you help me get it back and seventy-five of them are yours. Word."

That was all I needed to hear. Seventy-five bands was enough to help me and Jade float for a little while. She needed more clothes and so did I. We also had to shake Harlem. The last time I'd read one of the papers, her picture had been in there. The reward was up to seventy-five hundred now, it was crazy.

"Yo, let me go throw on them colors of darkness, kid, I'll be right back. Where your whip at?"

He nodded his head toward the window. "It's parked a block down. Yo, hurry up. I'm ready to splatter some shit, B, word is bond."

When I got into the bedroom, Jade was sitting on the edge of the bed with her head lowered. "Bentley, I don't have a good feeling about this."

Threw off my pants and slid into a pair of black ones, added the black Timbs and matching fatigue jacket. I got dressed as fast as I could and laced up my boots, before packing another Glock that matched the first one. "Got a bad feeling about what, Jade?" I knew she was about to get on the road of trying to stop me from going, but there was no way I could pass up seventy-five thousand dollars. For her and I, that was life-changing money. We could travel far with it, and do it comfortably.

"I don't think you should go with him this morning, Bentley. Something is going to happen. I can feel it deep in my bones. You cannot go with him, baby, please listen to me." She stood up and walked over to me, slid her arms around my waist.

I sighed, turned around to face her, and peeled her away from my body. "Baby, I can't leave my mans out on a limb like this. I gotta aid him. Gotta make sure don't nobody take advantage of him. He'd do the same for me. Plus, it's seventy-five bands in it for us. I can't pass that up. I'ma shoot out here to the Bronx and be right back, baby. Matter fact, you get dressed. I'ma take you shopping as soon as I get back. It's black Friday anyway."

She shook her head. "I don't care about shopping, Bentley. I care about you. I don't want you to leave me right now. Not again, not today. Please." She walked away from me and hugged herself.

I lowered my head. "Jade, I gotta get this money. I'll be right, right back. Don't think of it as me leaving you. Think of it as me doing what I gotta do for us." I kissed her cheeks and stepped into the hallway. "You own my heart, baby. I gotta make it happen for us. You deserve the best, Jade."

She turned her back to me so I couldn't see her face. "Just hurry back, Bentley. Please hurry back and be careful."

I nodded and was about to walk off, when she ran into the hallway and hugged me tight. "Damn it, Bentley, you got my heart too. I need you."

Her words caused me both to become weak and strong at the same time. They made me both afraid, and determined to do what I needed to do for us. "I'll be back, baby, you be dressed and ready to get anything that you want."

She smiled and nodded. "Okay. I will be. I'ma go get in the shower right now. You got me all sticky."

***

"Yo, son, you sure you ready?" Santana asked, placing his hand on the knob to the back door of the trap house we were set to run in. He had a Glock in his right hand and a ski mask over his face. Only minutes prior, his inside man had come out the back door and left it open for us, after confirming there were two men inside, along with Milan. The same two men that had robbed Santana were currently inside, counting the money they retrieved from him.

"Nigga, let's do this. It's Brooklyn, son, word up." I straightened my white ski mask, and nodded.

He nodded back, twisted the knob and rushed up the back steps, with me behind him ready to smoke somethin'. We ran into another door, which he swung open for me. I rushed inside with both Glocks brandished. The first thing I saw was Milan, standing in front of a refrigerator, drinking a bottle of apple juice. When the door opened, she dropped it and got ready to scream, but before she could emit a sound, I swung and the Glock caught her right across the chin, knocking her into the refrigerator, and out cold. The juice crashed to the floor, and rolled under the sink.

Santana rushed past me into the living room, where the two dudes were in there counting a table full of money. "You fuck niggas thought it was sweet. Gon try and play a don!" *Boom. Boom. Boom. Boom. Boom.*

His bullets ate up their flesh, before he pulled a black garbage bag out of his pants, and began to fill it with the money they'd stolen from him. "Yo, smoke that bitch too, B. Word is bond, ain't nobody walking out of here." He threw an extra garbage bag at me. "Hurry up and fill that bitch up."

I grabbed it and came to his side, putting as much money into the bag as I could, while he did the same thing beside me. My heart felt like it was about to burst, it was pounding so hard. We had to get the fuck out of there. After all the money was snatched up, I made my way to the back door and the way we'd come. "Let's go, nigga."

He ran behind me and paused in the kitchen, aimed his gun down at Milan. "Pretty bitch was a waste of flesh." *Boom. Boom. Boom.*

"Let's roll, kid."

We rushed out of the back door, and ran down the alley at full speed. When we got back to his truck, he pulled his connect that had been acting as a lookout, out of it and smoked him too. "Fuck nigga, I can't trust no snitch."

***

We rolled back to Harlem in silence. My mind was all over the place. I'd just watched the homie smoke four people as if it wasn't nothin'. That was eye opening to me. I had to get the fuck out of New York. The lifestyle was wild, and it was only a matter of time before I had a bunch of bodies under my belt like Santana. I was trying to avoid that. I knew life had more to offer than what the streets claimed it did. I wanted more for myself. More for Jade. We both deserved the best life had to offer.

Santana rolled past 143rd and Broadway and jerked his neck back. "Yo, who the fuck Twelve sweating like this?"

I perked up, scanning the scene. There were police cruisers everywhere, all across 143rd, and 144th. When we got to the corner of 145th where the trap was that me and Jade stayed in, the street was completely blocked off with barricades. I rubber necked to see if I could see our building, and did. There appeared to be at least four police cars parked in front of it, and a bunch of officers surrounding the building on foot. I felt my heart skip a beat. "Damn, Jade!"

To Be Continued...
Life of Sin 2
Coming Soon

Submission Guideline

Submit the first three chapters of your completed manuscript to ldpsubmissions@gmail.com, subject line: Your book's title. The manuscript must be in a .doc file and sent as an attachment. Document should be in Times New Roman, double spaced and in size 12 font. Also, provide your synopsis and full contact information. If sending multiple submissions, they must each be in a separate email.

Have a story but no way to send it electronically? You can still submit to LDP/Ca$h Presents. Send in the first three chapters, written or typed, of your completed manuscript to:

LDP: Submissions Dept
Po Box 870494
Mesquite, Tx 75187

DO NOT send original manuscript. Must be a duplicate.

Provide your synopsis and a cover letter containing your full contact information.

Thanks for considering LDP and Ca$h Presents.

BOW DOWN TO MY GANGSTA

By **Ca$h**

TORN BETWEEN TWO

By **Coffee**

BLOOD STAINS OF A SHOTTA **III**

By **Jamaica**

STEADY MOBBIN **III**

By **Marcellus Allen**

BLOOD OF A BOSS **V**

By **Askari**

LOYAL TO THE GAME **IV**

LIFE OF SIN II

By **T.J. & Jelissa**

A DOPEBOY'S PRAYER **II**

By **Eddie "Wolf" Lee**

IF LOVING YOU IS WRONG... **III**

LOVE ME EVEN WHEN IT HURTS **II**

By **Jelissa**

TRUE SAVAGE **VI**

By **Chris Green**

BLAST FOR ME **III**

A BRONX TALE

By **Ghost**

ADDICTIED TO THE DRAMA **III**

By **Jamila Mathis**

Life of Sin

LIPSTICK KILLAH **III**

CRIME OF PASSION **II**

By **Mimi**

WHAT BAD BITCHES DO **III**

KILL ZONE **II**

By **Aryanna**

THE COST OF LOYALTY **II**

By **Kweli**

SHE FELL IN LOVE WITH A REAL ONE **II**

By **Tamara Butler**

LOVE SHOULDN'T HURT **III**

RENEGADE BOYS **II**

By **Meesha**

CORRUPTED BY A GANGSTA **IV**

By **Destiny Skai**

A GANGSTER'S CODE **III**

By **J-Blunt**

KING OF NEW YORK III

By **T.J. Edwards**

CUM FOR ME **IV**

By **Ca$h & Company**

GORILLAS IN THE BAY

De'Kari

THE STREETS ARE CALLING

Duquie Wilson

KINGPIN KILLAZ II

Hood Rich

STEADY MOBBIN' **III**

Marcellus Allen

SINS OF A HUSTLA II

ASAD

HER MAN, MINE'S TOO **II**

Nicole Goosby

GORILLAZ IN THE BAY **II**

DE'KARI

TRIGGADALE II

Elijah R. Freeman

THE STREETS ARE CALLING **II**

Duquie Wilson

Available Now

RESTRAINING ORDER **I & II**

By **CA$H & Coffee**

LOVE KNOWS NO BOUNDARIES **I II & III**

By **Coffee**

RAISED AS A GOON I, II, III & IV

BRED BY THE SLUMS I, II, III

BLAST FOR ME I & II

ROTTEN TO THE CORE I III

By **Ghost**

LAY IT DOWN **I & II**

LAST OF A DYING BREED

BLOOD STAINS OF A SHOTTA I & II

Life of Sin

By **Jamaica**

LOYAL TO THE GAME

LOYAL TO THE GAME II

LOYAL TO THE GAME III

LIFE OF SIN

By **TJ & Jelissa**

BLOODY COMMAS I & II

SKI MASK CARTEL I II & III

KING OF NEW YORK I II

By **T.J. Edwards**

IF LOVING HIM IS WRONG…I & II

LOVE ME EVEN WHEN IT HURTS

By **Jelissa**

WHEN THE STREETS CLAP BACK I & II III

By **Jibril Williams**

A DISTINGUISHED THUG STOLE MY HEART I II & III

LOVE SHOULDN'T HURT I II

RENEGADE BOYS

By **Meesha**

A GANGSTER'S CODE I & II

By J-Blunt

PUSH IT TO THE LIMIT

By **Bre' Hayes**

BLOOD OF A BOSS **I, II, III & IV**

By **Askari**

THE STREETS BLEED MURDER **I, II & III**

THE HEART OF A GANGSTA I II& III

T.J. & Jelissa

By **Jerry Jackson**

CUM FOR ME

CUM FOR ME 2

CUM FOR ME 3

An **LDP Erotica Collaboration**

BRIDE OF A HUSTLA **I II & II**

THE FETTI GIRLS **I, II& III**

CORRUPTED BY A GANGSTA I, II & III

By **Destiny Skai**

WHEN A GOOD GIRL GOES BAD

By **Adrienne**

A GANGSTER'S REVENGE **I II III & IV**

THE BOSS MAN'S DAUGHTERS

THE BOSS MAN'S DAUGHTERS II

THE BOSSMAN'S DAUGHTERS III

THE BOSSMAN'S DAUGHTERS IV

THE BOSS MAN'S DAUGHTERS **V**

A SAVAGE LOVE **I & II**

BAE BELONGS TO ME

A HUSTLER'S DECEIT I, II

WHAT BAD BITCHES DO I, II

By **Aryanna**

A KINGPIN'S AMBITON

A KINGPIN'S AMBITION **II**

I MURDER FOR THE DOUGH

By **Ambitious**

TRUE SAVAGE

Life of Sin

TRUE SAVAGE II

TRUE SAVAGE **III**

TRUE SAVAGE **IV**

TRUE SAVAGE **V**

By **Chris Green**

A DOPEBOY'S PRAYER

By **Eddie "Wolf" Lee**

THE KING CARTEL **I, II & III**

By **Frank Gresham**

THESE NIGGAS AIN'T LOYAL **I, II & III**

By **Nikki Tee**

GANGSTA SHYT **I II &III**

By **CATO**

THE ULTIMATE BETRAYAL

By **Phoenix**

BOSS'N UP **I , II & III**

By **Royal Nicole**

I LOVE YOU TO DEATH

By Destiny J

I RIDE FOR MY HITTA

I STILL RIDE FOR MY HITTA

By **Misty Holt**

LOVE & CHASIN' PAPER

By **Qay Crockett**

TO DIE IN VAIN

By **ASAD**

BROOKLYN HUSTLAZ

T.J. & Jelissa

By **Boogsy Morina**
BROOKLYN ON LOCK I & II
By **Sonovia**
GANGSTA CITY
By **Teddy Duke**
A DRUG KING AND HIS DIAMOND I & II III
A DOPEMAN'S RICHES
HER MAN, MINE'S TOO
By **Nicole Goosby**
TRAPHOUSE KING **I II & III**   '
KINGPIN KILLAZ
By **Hood Rich**
LIPSTICK KILLAH **I, II**
CRIME OF PASSION
By **Mimi**
STEADY MOBBN' **I, II**
By **Marcellus Allen**
WHO SHOT YA **I, II**
Renta
GORILLAZ IN THE BAY
DE'KARI
TRIGGADALE
Elijah R. Freeman
GOD BLESS THE TRAPPERS I, II, III
THESE SCANDALOUS STREETS I, II, III
FEAR MY GANGSTA I, II
THESE STREETS DON'T LOVE NOBODY I, II

190

Life of Sin

Tranay Adams

THE STREETS ARE CALLING

Duquie Wilson

SINS OF A HUSTLA

ASAD

BOOKS BY LDP'S CEO, CA$H

TRUST IN NO MAN

TRUST IN NO MAN 2

TRUST IN NO MAN 3

BONDED BY BLOOD

SHORTY GOT A THUG

THUGS CRY

THUGS CRY 2

THUGS CRY 3

TRUST NO BITCH

TRUST NO BITCH 2

TRUST NO BITCH 3

TIL MY CASKET DROPS

RESTRAINING ORDER

RESTRAINING ORDER 2

IN LOVE WITH A CONVICT

Coming Soon

BONDED BY BLOOD 2

BOW DOWN TO MY GANGSTA